BITE ME AGAIN

NIGHTWOOD CLAN SERIES BOOK 1

HARPER DAKOTA

Warning:

This book contains mature themes and is intended to be read by ages 18+. There is mention of rape, that resulted in a child, to a non-primary character. Event was in the past and there is no graphic description. Serious illness of a main character occurs in plotline. Contains paranormal and magical themes, including fated mates. One couple mentioned in the book is a male/male couple.

Trademark Acknowledgements:

The author acknowledges the following trademarks and trademark status of these items mentioned in the book:

Epsom Salt

Ticket To Ride

Gardenscapes

Let's Get It On by Marvin Gaye

Keurig

BITE ME AGAIN

Born with an empathetic healing ability, Shaye's life has been filled with the rejection of people who didn't understand her gift. With only a few close friends, she lives a nomadic lifestyle as a traveling nurse.

Shaye knew she was different since she was a child, but never really understood it. When her latest assignment brings her to a small town in Tennessee, she never expected it to change her life. Spending a day exploring, her powers draw her to the large house on the outskirts of town. Shaye finds a man being tortured and uses her gifts to save him. As she recovers from healing him, she discovers that she is his fated mate. Growing up human, her worldview is blown wide open when she is introduced to a world where magic and paranormal creatures exist, including vampires, werewolves, and Fae.

Her mate, Rolf, is caring and protective. Although Shaye saved him once, he is still in danger. His father wants to either use him for his power or kill him if he resists. With multiple attempts to end Rolf's life, can Shaye, Rolf, and their friends defeat this monster or will their love end before it fully begins?

PROLOGUE

S haye had always been able to sense things others couldn't. She could sense when people were in pain, everything from a simple papercut to someone dying. As a child, her parents encouraged, well, really forced, her to hide her abilities. They thought it was unnatural. Her mother had blamed it on her being born on Halloween at the witching hour. As she grew older, she tried researching to find out more about herself, her abilities, how to control them. From what she could tell based on her research, she thought she was a sort of empath, mostly dealing with healing and a dash of telepathy thrown in. The telepathy was extremely weak. She could feel others' pain when she was close to them but could only pick up on someone's pain from far away if they were really projecting. She didn't seem to have any other telepathic gifts, no reading people's thoughts or talking to other people in their minds.

Unfortunately, when she was younger there had been no one there to teach her to shield herself, so she felt people's pain every day unless she was extremely isolated. As she grew older, she felt that she had been given this gift for a reason and intended to help as many as she could. At age eighteen, her parents pushed her out of their home. She found a temporary home in New Orleans where she attended LSU for nursing. Shaye had been lucky enough that her friend from high school had left with her; they both attended LSU and they had supported each other through college. It was the New Orleans culture that enabled her to embrace her gifts. She was able to make a few contacts that taught her the basics of shielding herself and even gained a few close friends. It also helped that New Orleans had so many gifted people living there that could shield themselves, so she was surrounded by at least a little bumper of protection from their pain.

After graduation, she felt a calling to leave her adopted hometown and became a traveling nurse. Most places didn't have as many gifted people as New Orleans, so it was hard to stay in one place for too long if there was a high population density. Even with the basic shields, the pain could become overwhelming. Once it became too much, or people began to notice how quickly her patients improved, she would move on. People often feared what they did not understand, and she didn't want to attract too much attention. She had made a few friends on her travels across the country and kept in touch with them as often as she could. Some were normal people who simply accepted the extraordinary, others had unusual skills like she did. Each one brought some-thing new to her life and kept her grounded when she thought the pain of the world would drive her insane. They had all grown adept at shielding themselves from her and were the only ones she could be near at times.

Today was looking to be a good day. She had about a week off before starting her new job and had managed to get a full night's sleep and meditated enough that her minor shields were in place again. There was an outdoor market with a new coffee shop that she was eager to try. Eventually, her shields would start to wear down again. It wasn't often that she got a day like this, so she intended to enjoy it for as long as it lasted.

However, fate seemed to have a different agenda for her today.

1

She was window shopping at the bookstore, trying to decide if she could fit another book on her desk. Right now, she was living out of a local hotel until she found an apartment to rent, so she didn't have a lot of space. If she double stacked them, then she would definitely have room for that new series in the window. Suddenly, a gut-wrenching pain hit her, doubling her over in agony. She felt the sweat run down her face, her eyes so sensitive to the light they seemed to burn, tears running down her cheeks. The pain was almost more than she could bear and remain sane.

"Miss? Are you alright? Do you need me to call someone?" she heard a voice ask, concerned.

She could only shake her head. Her throat was so closed up, she could barely breathe.

Soon the pain was bearable enough that she could stand up. She managed to walk using the building as support. She knew the pain was not her own. It felt like someone was projecting and looking for help. They were in some of the worst agony she had ever felt.

She followed her instincts and the trail of pain to the

mansion on the outskirts of town. As she got closer to the house, the pain was joined by a sense of evil nearby. It wasn't coming from the person she was trying to help, but another entity.

She had heard that the owner of this property was a bit of a recluse, but she could see that the house and its grounds had been well maintained. She had never ventured too close to the house, not wanting to invade their privacy. The closest she got was driving by on her way to somewhere else or walking by on one of her longer walks. The structure sat far back from the road, the long driveway giving it a stately feel. It was a large two-story stone house, mansion-sized, with wide entry steps leading up to a massive set of wood and metal doors. There was a turret on either side of the front entry, but those seemed to be the only level on the third floor. Climbing up the front steps, she paused, unsure of her next steps.

'*Go to the top floor, the left turret,*' she heard a female voice whisper urgently to her. Turning her head, she saw that there was no one there. She only hoped that this was not a sign of her losing her mind, or even of a new power developing. She had her hands full with the one she already had. She walked up to the front door, ignoring the warnings her senses were giving to her. The front door was open—not a good sign.

'*Get away. There is evil here. Run,*' she heard another voice urge her as she stepped across the threshold. This time, the rush of adrenaline had nothing to do with fear, and everything to do with the deep husky sound of his voice.

'*Please, you must help him, or he will die! Save him for me,*' she heard the first voice whisper anxiously, fearfully. It sounded as though a mother was talking.

"I will try," she whispered back. Looking around the

entry of the house, it was clearly lived in. There was furniture, window dressings, and not a speck of dust in sight.

Drawing her shields around her as much as she was able and hoping they would hold, she climbed up the flights of stairs. She finally stopped at a door on the third level. The door was shut but she could feel two people inside. She could feel waves of agony coming from the room and her breath froze in her chest for a moment.

Taking a deep breath, holding her phone ready to call 911, she pushed open the door. There were two people inside, one tied to a chain hanging from the ceiling and the other man leaning over him. The standing man was classically handsome, probably around six feet tall with dark brown hair and hazel eyes, his build was leanly muscled. However, as he turned toward her, his hazel eyes were cold and lacking any joy or life. The evil energy was emanating out of him.

'*Evil,*' she heard the woman's voice hiss with hatred in her tone.

"Ah, another plaything for me," he said as he began to move toward her with manic anticipation in his eyes. The constrained man growled and tried to grab at the other man. He merely laughed at him and said "another time" before vanishing out the window. Shaye rushed to the man tied to the ceiling, intent on finding a way to get him down. He was barely able to stand, the chains holding him up. They were wrapped around his wrists and neck with a lock at his throat. The hook the chain was attached to was too high for her to reach unless she could find a ladder.

'*Cover the windows first,*' she heard him whisper. His was the voice that had warned her away.

After following his directions and drawing the curtains over the windows, she hurried back to him. She stared in horror at his body. He was wearing a pair of pants, but nothing else. His legs were tied together with wire at the ankles. He had probably been handsome before the thing had gotten to him. His body was sculpted with well-formed muscles, but it was now battered beyond anything she had ever seen. His ice-blue eyes were now reddened to the point where she could not see any white left in them. Tears were running from both eyes, but it seemed more of a bodily reaction than crying. His face had been beaten and cut, blood was streaming in little rivers from his face and mouth. His dark hair was wet with sweat, and it looked like there was blood mixed in as well. The rest of his body fared the same, although it looked like someone had also used a whip on him. There were burn marks scattered over his torso and back.

She started at his feet and unwound the wire holding his ankles together. The wire had cut into his skin. His left leg was badly bruised and she sensed a break.

"I need to call an ambulance," she told him as she tried to find a way to get him out of the chains. She was not sure if she could heal all his wounds on her own; she had never attempted this depth of injuries by herself.

'No. Just leave me be,' she heard him say. He must have some sort of telepathic power she decided. He had not used his mouth to speak. She could also understand why he would not want to be subjected to a hospital, if this was the case.

"Alright, no hospital," she agreed. "But I cannot leave you here like this. I have to find some way to get you down and then I can help." The chains were wrapped tight, she couldn't find any wiggle room to get his hands out.

'There is a key in my back pocket.'

"Why is it in your pocket?" she asked incredulously.

'He left it there to taunt me, that escape was so close, but I couldn't reach it with the chains around my neck.'

"Okay, once I get this unlocked and the chains loose, try to lean on me. It looks like your leg is broken. Since you're some sort of telepath, you might understand what I am a little better than most people would. I can heal, so I'm going to try to heal you as much as I can. It would be better if you could be on a bed or a couch though," she said. "Is there one close by?"

'Basement.'

"I don't think I am strong enough to get you all the way down there." She stood still for a moment, worrying her lip as she tried to decide the best course of action. During the healing process, the bed was as much for his comfort, as it was for her own. She would just have to try to heal him enough here and then try to move him later, she decided. Maybe she could find some pillows and a blanket for the floor, she thought as she got the last of the chain unwrapped from him. She braced herself to take his weight, it was a little awkward trying to hold him up as he was probably almost a foot taller than her.

"I'm going to lay you down on the floor," she told him as she slipped her arms around his waist to support his weight. The air seemed to shimmer and get misty. She blinked to clear her eyes and she opened them to find herself in what looked like a basement.

"Well, I guess you have another ability. That certainly was useful, but you should not have wasted your strength," she scolded. "Alright, there's the bed. That's not too far to make it." She felt the air move again. "No! Do not do that. It will only make it harder for me, the weaker you are." She still did not know if she could heal him as it was.

After a few painfully slow steps, they reached the bed.

"Here we are, lie down," she told him, seeing him

watching her. She bent down and took her sandals off, digging her toes into the shaggy charcoal and navy carpet covering the floor. "This probably is not the best place for you, but at least you'll be comfortable if you won't go to the hospital. I'm going to try to heal you as much as I can. It helps if you relax and don't push against it. Afterward, you will probably fall asleep. If I use a lot of energy, I may pass out," she told him. If this does not kill me first, she added to herself. If she had any sense left in her she would be calling an ambulance instead of trying this on her own. But she felt connected to him somehow. She was meant to be here. She **had** to save him.

"I know this is awkward for both of us, but I need to see how much it hurt you," she told him as she started to remove his pants. Once he was in just his boxer briefs, she straightened his broken leg to make the healing easier on both of them. She focused on feeling outside her body, searching out his injuries. His whole body was a mass of damage and pain. The injuries ranged from hours old to days old. His leg was broken, as were some of the bones in his arms. The muscles in his arms were damaged from hanging from the ceiling. The cuts and burns along his body varied in size and shape, some were only surface wounds, but others went bone deep. She began healing the worst ones first. He had lost a lot of blood and she wanted to get the blood loss under control. She found a small amount of internal bleeding. There was a small crack in his skull and the concussion to go with it. Shaye was puzzled over why she had not sensed him in pain before today. She had been in town and should have been able to sense this amount of damage. He must have some sort of shield, she realized.

His body was different than any other person that she had healed. Being linked to someone during the healing sometimes allowed her to see glimpses of their lives, the type of person they really were. This man confused her. She could see love in his past, but also flashes of horrendous violence. She could also detect a lingering sense of the evil that had done this to him, as if this wasn't the first time they had met.

She could feel herself tiring quickly. She had no idea how much time had passed. There are only the cuts on his face left, I can do this, she encouraged herself, pushing the creeping blackness away. There was something he was trying to keep from her. She finished up healing his face and concentrated on his secret. She did not want to miss anything that needed to be healed. His resistance was strong, but she pushed past it with the last of her strength. She sensed that she never would have been able to do it if he was at his full strength.

"No. It can't be," she whispered. One word remained in her mind as she slid into the darkness that had been waiting to claim her. It was a darkness she was not sure she would wake up from.

Vampire.

2

Rolfston sat up, careful of his newly mended bones and skin. He would have healed eventually. Probably. He was grateful for her speeding up the process, but she had found out his secret. He had been too weak to keep it from her. He was surprised she had not run away in horror, he thought, as he turned toward her. He immediately began cursing in his native language.

Her body lay at an odd angle from where she had collapsed, dark shadows under her eyes and her skin deathly pale. As he moved her more fully onto the bed, he could hear her breathing start to labor and her heart slow down. She had used too much of herself to heal him and now her body was shutting down.

Taking her to a hospital was out of the question; he didn't think they had the time. He gathered her in his arms and took her to an upstairs room. With just a thought, the blinds closed and the candles placed around the room were lit. This room normally acted as his meditation room. There was much peace to be found in this quiet room. The bed from the basement appeared, covered in clean sheets. Laying her on the bed, he spoke to her in her mind.

"You've healed me, little one, at too great an expense to yourself. It is now time to return the favor the only way I can. I only pray that you can understand." He sat behind her, pulling her into his lap, cradling her. Extending his fangs, he used one to cut his wrist and pressed it to her lips. "Drink. Drink and heal." Rolfston made sure she drank just enough to ensure that she would live and heal. He licked the wound closed on his wrist and laid her down on the bed.

'*You are going to stay put and watch over her. Do not even contemplate going out. The first thing you should do is reset the safeguards,*' a concerned but irritated voice scolded.

'*Yes, Mother,*' he sighed. There was an ocean between them and she still nagged.

'*I am not joking. You need to protect her. She is utterly defenseless.*'

'*I just did,*' he muttered in his own defense.

'*No, you helped her to heal her body. My son, I have been around on this earth longer than you have. Granted, you have been immortal a little longer, but I still have more experience than you have. Whether you see it yet or not, there is something there between you,*' she insisted.

'*What have you seen?*' he asked resigned. His mother was famous in their family for having visions, but only telling what she deemed appropriate.

'*She is your destiny, your mate. You both need each other; neither can exist fully without the other.*'

'*What else is there?*' He knew she was holding back.

'*It is not for you to know yet. Time will reveal it to you. It could be disastrous if you find out too soon. Some things are meant to be in their own time.*'

Rolfston sighed. It would be of no use to argue with

her; he knew she spoke the truth. *'Mother? I would ask your help.'*

'You need only ask.'

'My strength is not quite back all the way. Would you help me with the safeguards?'

'Go and feed. You will need your strength,' she replied.

He hesitated before answering. *'I will later.'* He felt compelled to keep this girl safe.

'Rest then. I will make sure you both are safe.'

Rolfston lay beside the sleeping girl. He gazed at her face, feeling drawn to her. As his eyes skimmed over her wavy brown hair, he found himself remembering her compassionate gray eyes. She had been much shorter than him, probably around five foot four. He was curious as to the type of person who would risk her own well-being to save others. For the moment, they were connected through the blood exchange. He wanted to explore her mind more, but he had other things that were more pressing. She would doubtless wake up with questions. Looking into her mind would require little to no strength; her defenses and barriers would be weakened while she slept. Now that his body was no longer in constant pain and the scent of his own blood had faded, he could pick up hints of her unique scent. Taking a deep breath, he realized that his mother was correct when she said they were linked together, as his instincts shouted MATE! He wanted to know who Fate had chosen for him as a mate and allowed himself to close his eyes and relax, letting her memories become his own.

He saw her birth, her parents joy at finally having a child after waiting for one for so long. He saw her crying because she could not heal a cat she had found after it had been hit by a car. Her parents' joy turning to fear when they saw her "differences." The friends she had made through the years abandoning her when they discovered she was different. The recent friends who loved and accepted her for who she was, the ones that helped her when the world was too much for her to handle alone. The pain she felt through him, because of him. When he got to her most recent move to town, he saw her weariness and yearning for someplace to settle down, and her love of his house. That made him smile.

He was worried about his father now knowing of her existence. She had helped save him, so his father would take that to mean she was against him. Rolf knew that his father would love to mess with her, to try to gain access to her innocence and healing abilities, just to destroy her. He may even want to turn her for himself, Rolfston realized. She was strong though, attempting to heal the world when she could, not in the least way attracted to evil. She now had people who would love and protect her, himself and his friends included. Rolfston would not allow anything to happen to her. He let himself sleep beside her, knowing he would awaken before she did. His mother's safeguards would hold as they rested.

3

It was three days before she woke. For three days he studied her, learned about her, slept beside her, and worried for her. He had not known she would sleep for so long. Rolfston could feel her warring with herself. Her body was announcing its desire to wake up, her mind did not want to face what had happened. He watched her open her eyes, wariness in them already. Her body tensing, ready to run if need be.

"Where am I?"

"In my house. You've been sleeping for three days," he added, watching her beautiful gray eyes widen.

"I've never slept that long. I almost thought…" that I would not come back, she added silently to herself.

"You almost didn't," Rolf answered her unspoken thought. He could hear her through their bond. "You were dying. It was stupid of you to try to heal that many injuries," he said. Truth be told, he was afraid. In the last few days, he had fallen in love with her through their connection. She had almost died before he could really know her.

"How did you know what I was thinking?"

"It is one of my many talents."

"I *was* dying. Why didn't I?"

"I can help heal in my own way," he answered, not sure if he should tell her the whole truth. She had not remembered his secret yet. Rolfston sat on the edge of the bed, watching her think it through, trying to recapture her memories, seeing the look on her face when she remembered.

"You're a— Why did you keep me here?" she asked, panicked now that she remembered.

"You needed time to heal. I won't harm you; I can't harm you." He didn't elaborate. She was not ready to hear that part yet. She surprised him by grabbing his wrist. Her eyes lost their focus as she concentrated. He looked down and the red line had disappeared.

"I drank from there. You gave to me to save me, but you did not heal yourself all the way. Why?"

"It would have taken too much energy. At this point, I only have a limited supply. I haven't recovered all the way yet." It was his own fault. He had not wanted to leave her alone, not even for him to go down to the kitchen to get some bagged blood.

"Who was the woman I heard?"

"My mother."

"Is she here?"

"No. She lives in Europe at the moment."

"Oh." She was having a hard time trying to understand all of this. The only thing she knew for certain was that he was a vampire, he had saved her life, and he spoke the truth when he vowed to not harm her. She was not sure how she knew, only that her instincts told her to trust him.

"My mother and I can speak to each other telepathically no matter where we are," he added.

"Why could I hear you?"

Rolfston did not want to lie to her, but he wanted her to know only if she was ready. "If you really want to know, you only have to look. We are bonded now through your healing and the exchange."

"But we were somehow linked before that."

"It seems as if Fate deemed it that way," he agreed.

"Am I…" She didn't know how to ask.

"No. I did not turn you to become like me."

"What do you want from me?"

"To get to know you. Fate has a plan for us, but I know humans do not put much stock in Fated mates. I can settle for getting to know each other slowly."

"I have things I have to do," she began. She did feel drawn to him, had since the moment she heard his voice, but this was happening too fast and it frightened her.

"You still can, but I will go with you. Not to hinder you, but to protect you. I can walk or drive you to work, make sure you get home safely."

"Protect me from what?" she asked, uncertain.

"*He* is still out there waiting. I won't let him have you."

"*He?*"

"What you call evil—the man you saw earlier." He could see the question in her mind before she voiced it. "He wants me because I will not submit to him. He will not stop until he doesn't view me as a threat any longer. He would see me dead."

"Which is what he was trying to do," Shaye stated.

"Maybe. I think he was trying to get his message across this time. He promised the pain would stop if I went far away and left this area to him alone. I really don't like the fact that he noticed you."

"Why would he want me?" she asked confused.

"I'm only guessing that he would, but he's always

been vindictive. You helped me, which means you didn't help him—"

"Because he was hurting you!" Shaye interrupted. "I could feel the evil coming from him. There is no way that I would have helped him instead."

"He likes to corrupt people, to make them join him. If he could turn you and get you to follow him, he would gain access to your healing. When you are a huge asshole, it's always a plus to have a healer in your corner. As far as I know, he doesn't have one yet."

"Who is he?" Shaye asked.

Rolfston hissed an angry breath. He had to calm himself when he saw her backing away from him. "I won't harm you; I swear it on all I hold dear. He is Vladimir, my maker. My father. Sperm donor is a closer description. He was never around when I was young and human. I am very grateful for that."

"I don't understand," she replied, moving back toward him. She didn't fear him, he had just surprised her.

Rolfston did not want to relive the pain of his younger memories, but she deserved an explanation. She would only trust him and hopefully in time grow to love him, if he was honest with her. She was so quiet that he thought she had fallen asleep again, but then he felt her in his mind exploring his memories.

She touched his head, concentrating on their bond. She could see that speaking about it caused him pain, so she decided to look in his mind instead. What she found there fascinated her. She saw his happy childhood with his mother, his growing up to adulthood. She saw the day *he* came and tore out his throat, converting him against his will.

Rolfston grabbed her hands. "That's enough. You are going to exhaust yourself." If he were being honest with himself, there were things he did not want her to see yet. He had kept some memories to himself. There was no need for her to see everything revolting in his life all at once. There was a time where he desperately wanted his father's approval and did things that he was not proud of, things he was ashamed that he had allowed to happen. That was, until he learned the truth of his "father" and walked away.

"Why are you still weak?" she asked, worried.

"I'll be better once I feed and rest some more."

"So, you're not really immortal?"

"Not very many things that I know of are. We just live a very, very long time. We can starve to death slowly, losing our strength for years upon years until we die. Another vampire can kill us." He grinned at the thoughts running through her mind. "Sunlight is only uncomfortable if we are already weakened. Garlic is delicious. Most of the things that can kill us, will kill anyone: stake through the heart, decapitation, burning. We are no more flammable than anyone else but burning our bodies completely will make sure we can't heal. We do have faster healing, so we can withstand quite a bit before we would die."

"You still had days old injuries when I found you," Shaye stated, confused.

"If we aren't able to drink and replenish what we lost in addition to what we need to heal, the process can become extremely slow. I hadn't been able to drink in days, and had been damaged enough for long enough, that the injures were slow to heal." Rolf answered.

"What do we do now?"

Rolfston felt his heartbeat quicken when she said "we." "First I think we should introduce ourselves." He smiled. "I'm Rolfston."

"Shaye," she replied nervously. She could not believe

this was all happening to her. She led a very quiet life; this was going to change everything, her instincts told her. He spoke the truth; Fate had decided for them already. It was only a matter of them surrendering to it. She had always made her own choices, having part of that taken away was disconcerting.

"I would like for you to move in here with me. I will be able to watch over you better and we would be able to get to know one another."

After a little bit of discussion, she eventually agreed to move into the mansion. She had only been living out of a hotel room as it was, but it was happening much faster than her mind wanted to process now. Rolfston assured her that they would sleep in different beds and even different floors until she chose otherwise. He usually slept in the basement where there was little chance anyone could surprise him while he slept. He offered to have someone deliver furniture for her so that she could have her own room. Seeing her hesitation, Rolfston added that they could go out shopping for things instead if she wanted.

She saw in his eyes, even felt along their bond, that he was keeping something from her. She had a feeling that he would not tell her if it would affect her decision, so she looked instead. Having this bond would come in handy. *'It will weaken you even more if we leave and you have to shield us from him sensing us,'* she thought to him.

Rolfston was amazed that she had spoken mentally to him without being taught. He and his mother had broadcasted their thoughts earlier so that she could hear them. It normally took a lot of skill to learn to project/speak quietly into someone else's mind, but she had accomplished it all on her own.

She could feel the pride he had in her. It amazed her at how warm and loved it made her feel. It had been a long while since someone had let her know they were proud of her. She knew her friends loved and accepted her, were amazed by her gifts, but it was somehow different coming from him. He smiled and she could feel a hand stroke her hair, even though he had not touched her.

'There are many ways to communicate, love,' he told her. *'And you are right, going out of my borders here would drain me more. I have help while I am on my property. This is my home, as such we are more protected, I am stronger. The warding is in place to keep him out for a while longer. My mother helped reinforce the safeguards after he left. I had been lazy about reinforcing them and he found a weak spot. Her love is a strong power to keep them in place until I can redo them. If we went out, I would have to shield us and it might drain my strength.'*

'Let's have someone deliver the furniture here. Could someone get my things from the hotel? What about food?' She felt awful mentioning food to him when he mentioned having to feed soon. It slipped out before she could catch it.

'Don't ever be afraid to ask anything of me or tell me. I need to fulfill your needs. I will drink later. I have someone I trust in town that will deliver everything we need. He will bring it here tonight. Do you want a tour of your new home in the meantime?' He sent a quick text to his friend to see if he could help with bringing things to the house.

She nodded, excited. She had always loved this place when she had gone by it during the short time she had been in town. It had called to her. Of course, now she knew that it was this man, not the house, that had drawn her here. She placed her hand trustingly into the one he held out.

Rolfston looked at her, amazed at how a simple question had caused her to cheer up. Her whole face was lit up by her eager grin. She looked like a child at Christmas, all hope and eagerness. He decided she needed to be spoiled, pampered, and doted on. She had not had enough of it in her life.

'I made some modifications when I bought this place. It may take you a while to remember all of the tricks,' he told her.

She nodded, concentrating on remembering all the things he showed her.

"This can be your room, if you would like, but I think there is another one that you will like much better. I'll save that for last," he teased her. He wanted to speak aloud so that he could hear her voice. She also had just healed, and he did not want her to wear herself out again. Physically she was healed, but he saw how much mental strength and energy it took from her to heal someone.

Shaye was amazed at how large everything was. Dark woods, cooler paint colors, and earth-tone tapestries decorated the rooms. She didn't see a lot of personal touches though, no pictures of his family, no plants. Everything seemed so old-fashioned, medieval almost, in décor.

Rolfston laughed at her thoughts. "You can change things if you want. I just liked how it looked. I grew up in the Georgian and Victorian periods and had no desire to live in it again." He laughed.

"I like it. It just needs a few brighter colors. You need some light around you. I think you've kept yourself hidden away in the dark too long."

'That may be, love, but now I have you,' he whispered in her mind seductively.

"I'll keep you on your toes," she promised.

The tour lasted a couple hours. They started in the basement, where it was just some storage, his bedroom and bathroom, and an exercise room. As they walked up to the main floor he said, "This floor is where most of the living spaces are. The second floor is all bedrooms and bathrooms." He told her every secret and trick to the rooms. He had hidden staircases and passageways, even ones that held secret hiding places in the passageways. His study was filled with the newest, top-of-the-line technology. "This currently works as my home office."

"What do you do for work?" Shaye asked curiously.

"I've been around a long time, so I've done a little bit of many things. Other than this house, I tend to be a saver, so I built up a nice nest egg. I was also able to get a nice collection of collectibles over the years, including some good investments. Currently, I manage those investments and some newer ones. I do a little day trading as well."

The next room had her almost jumping in excitement. It looked like they were in the turret, the front of the room was rounded. Bookshelves reached from the floor all the way to the third-floor ceiling, complete with a rolling ladder along the sides. There was a spiral staircase to the side of the room, leading to a third floor. The room was her every (almost) desire come true. This was by far her favorite room in the house.

"I've always wanted one of these," she admitted to him.

Well, he had just inadvertently discovered a way to woo her. "It's one of my favorite places as well. This is in the right turret and the books go all the way to the top. There is a railing up there for safety, but at the top there is a reading nook that I love to sit in during storms. It gives a great view overlooking the front of the house. Feel free to change anything. I want you to feel at home here. Everything I have is yours."

She glanced at him. "Some Chesterfield-style leather couches would be nice, something large enough to snuggle on," she suggested. There were some wingback chairs, but those probably weren't too comfortable for longer reading sessions. She couldn't wait to check out the reading nook.

"I'll have a couple brought in," he promised. "I think you'll like the next room too." He already knew she loved cooking, so she should like the kitchen. He was not creative in the kitchen. He normally just made simple meals or relied on take-out and microwave meals. Last year, for some unknown reason, he had the urge to completely update the kitchen. Now he knew why; it was for her. He was not disappointed when he saw her reaction.

"This is perfect! It has everything. It will make feeding my friends much easier when they come—" She suddenly stopped. She had somehow already accepted permanently staying here without admitting it to herself. Maybe she had jumped ahead too far, assuming it would be okay to have her friends here.

Rolfston watched as the emotions shown on her face changed from joy to uncertainty and wariness. He sighed. "This is your home now. Your friends will always be welcome."

He was rewarded with one of her smiles. It was all he needed. He could sense her getting tired already, so he decided to finish up the tour so she could rest. "We have one last room to see and then you need to rest."

As he led her upstairs into her bedroom, she could only stand there and stare. It was an enormous room with a window looking out onto the mountains and nearby creek. The closet itself was bigger than any room she had ever had in her whole life. She would need more clothes to even fill up a quarter of it, she laughed to herself.

'And I would be happy to help you with that,' he told her, his voice husky with desire. "Come into the bathroom. I

think there should be everything you need here," he told her as he led her into the room.

The walls were decorated in different shades of blue and gray, her favorite colors. The room had a feminine feel to it though. There was a Jacuzzi bath, a separate shower, candles everywhere, and a speaker set up on the far wall. "How did you…?" she asked, stunned.

"My mother designed the room. She has visions and last year told me that I needed to make this room. She even sent me a paint scheme and a rough design so that I would get it just right," he explained. "I will go call to check on the furniture if you want to take a bath or anything."

"I would love to take a bath," she exclaimed. "I feel a little scuzzy," she said with a laugh.

"Enjoy," he replied and made himself turn around and leave before he rushed things with her. Just the thought of her naked caused his body to leap readily to attention.

She was a little hurt with the curt exit. She thought they had been getting along well. Looking around the room, she found everything she needed in the cupboards and had just climbed in the tub when she felt him in her mind.

'I could not stay in there any longer. I promised you time and I was trying to honor that. The thought of you in the bath was too arousing. It does not help knowing that you are in the tub, naked, with only a door between us.'

'One day we'll share a bath together. I'm just not ready yet,' she promised him. She felt his lips brush across hers as she closed her eyes and relaxed. She simply smiled when she heard soothing music begin to play and the smell of aromatherapy candles filled the room. *'I could get used to this,'* she thought to him, *'but you should not be wasting your energy.'*

'It does not take much at all. Besides, I enjoy doing it for you.'

She leaned her head back against the edge of the tub and allowed the hot water to relax her. The music and the heat of the water had almost lured her to sleep when she heard some noises outside the door. *'Rolfston?'* she called to him anxiously.

'It is alright, love. Some of your furniture has arrived. Stay in there while we get it set up. Lean your head back and relax, I will not let any harm come to you,' he assured her.

It made her feel safe, just knowing he was looking out for her. She was enjoying the feeling of being cherished, of being loved, by him. It was all still scary with their future being haunted by an evil man, but she had to have faith that they would find some way to defeat him. It would be too cruel if Fate had shown her what could be her forever love and then took it away. She refused to accept that as an outcome. She was a healer and had just patched him up, she was falling in love with him already, she would not let him die.

Her fingers and toes began to prune, telling her it was time to get out. She took her time drying off, massaging the lotion into her tired skin.

'I can give you a foot rub tonight,' she heard him offer.

It was nice to be pampered, she thought to herself as she put on the soft robe that was waiting for her. Walking out of the bath, she listened as he let the movers out of the house. She saw her suitcases stacked along a wall. The bed was king-sized, a black wrought iron frame similar to a style that she had always wanted but never had the room for.

"Thank you," she said as he came back into the room. She did not know how he had managed to pull this all off.

"You're welcome. I know it's just a bed right now, but

I have a few more things coming in the morning. My friend needed a little bit more time for the rest of the items. Do you want to eat now, sleep some more, or I can give you that massage?" he suggested.

She allowed the robe to slide to the floor as she climbed onto the bed to lie on her stomach. Rolfston came back with lotion warming in his hands. He had wonderful hands she realized as he began to rub her; they were strong, very sculpted and masculine. They were the hands every woman fantasized about roaming over her body. Her muscles relaxed as he rubbed the tension out of them, but other areas began tensing in anticipation. With her eyes closed, she could fantasize to her heart's content about what those hands would do to her.

Shaye was too relaxed to keep from projecting all her thoughts. Rolfston groaned as he caught glimpses of her fantasies. He drew in the scent of her heat into his body. His cock hardened and pressed insistently against the front of his pants. He took a deep, slow breath to gain control over his own hormones and slowly let his hands roam lower over her body. Over her shoulders, down the curve of her back, and the swell of her ass. He let her get used to his hands on her inner thighs before he allowed his fingers to trail slowly over her lips, teasing her hidden bud until she moaned. Rolfston was in her mind, feeling what she felt through their bond. He could feel her arousal, the rush of liquid between her legs as he teased her. Her hips started to rise up and thrust back lightly against his fingers. He gave in to her silent demands, thrusting his fingers deep into her welcoming body. Her hips moved, helplessly grinding against him. He wanted to see her face as she orgasmed, so he flipped her over while keeping one hand deep within her body. Looking down into her face, her eyes were unfocused, and her lips parted as she panted, striving for the ultimate goal. Kissing her forehead, he scooted further down the bed and lowered his head, his tongue teasing her clit, tasting her, as his fingers slid in and out of her wet heat. His cock swelled painfully behind the zipper, but he kept control over himself. This time was just for her. He rubbed her clit harder with his tongue and sped up his thrusts until she grabbed hold of his hair and screamed out in completion.

Shaye felt wonderful, dazed, and floating on a rush of endorphins. She tugged at his wrist, bringing him up to lie beside her. '*Thank you*,' she told him sleepily.

'*You are very welcome*.' He felt inanely proud of himself for providing her with what she had craved. His own body was demanding attention, but her comfort was more important than his own. She needed time to adjust to the possibility of them being mates before they could have sex. Sex would only bind them further together, and she didn't need that until she had gotten to know him better and would accept him as her mate. For now, she needed sleep and then some food.

Rolfston wandered down to his room. Bending down to grab a bag of blood from his small bedroom refrigerator, he still felt a little weak. He would prefer to find something fresh, but Shaye was still recovering and he didn't want to leave her alone. It also felt like a betrayal somehow. He often didn't have sex with a live donor, but it was generally a pleasurable experience for them. He would heat up the bagged blood and talk to Shaye about it later.

This was not how he saw his night ending this morning. Just a few days ago, when his father caught him unawares outside of his home and knocked him out, Rolf had not expected to walk away from the encounter so easily. It was all thanks to his mate coming to his aid that he survived the experience with his father.

Although his house had been warded against unwanted visitors, the wards had only sensed that he was coming home and didn't differentiate between walking on his own and being dragged back in. By dragging his body across the property line, his father had been able to get onto the grounds and in the house. Rolf woke to find himself chained up and attached to the ceiling. At first it was a few punches and listening to his father's diatribe. His father believed that eventually Rolfston would want to control more land and gather a Clan of his own together. Although Rolf had a few friends scattered around the world that he would like to see more often, he wasn't extremely driven to form his own Clan. He tried explaining, again, that he was content in his home, in his chosen hometown. He loved meeting the people in town and watching over them from his home. That was when his father lost it; he saw humans as food, as playthings, something to use. Even if he changed them, he kept them under his control, only using them to add to his own power. The fact that Rolf wouldn't join him and support his "conquest efforts" was like an infected splinter, always there and growing more bothersome. He couldn't see that Rolfston was mostly content with his life how it was. He never wanted this fight his father created between them.

His mother had sensed his pain when the whips and fire came into play and he accidently let his mental shields drop for a moment. He made her promise to stay in Europe. His mother was much safer there, far away from Vladimir. Rolfston had moved to America many, many years ago to find new adventures. He had grown to love his new home and didn't want to leave it, nor did he want to leave the area completely to Vlad's mercy. He managed to keep his town safe from his father and his friends also knew to keep Vladimir from getting a stronghold on their towns as well.

He shook himself out of his ruminations. He grimaced as he drank the now lukewarm drink. Shaye should be waking up soon, he sensed, so he needed to place an order for food. She was bound to be hungry and would need the food to refuel all the energy she had used. He wasn't very familiar with her likes and dislikes though, so he placed an order for a few different types of pizza, a pasta dish, a salad, and of course breadsticks. What heathen ordered pizza without breadsticks?

About forty-five minutes later, the wards let him know someone was at the gate and he stepped out to meet the pizza delivery driver. Back inside, he gathered some plates and napkins, cups of water, and set the table. As soon as he finished putting out the silverware, he heard Shaye come down the stairs.

"Something smells really good," she said sleepily.

"It's just some pizza from my favorite place in town. I didn't have much in way of groceries," he replied.

She paused at the table when she saw two place settings. "Are you eating too?" she asked.

"If that's alright? Unless you would rather eat alone," Rolfston offered.

"No! I just wasn't sure if you ate real food. I thought you just drank blood," she answered sheepishly.

"I can eat and drink regular food, but I need the blood to live. Most of my nutrition comes from the blood, the food and other drinks are more for enjoyment and fitting in. I only have to drink blood about once or twice a month. I can drink it more often, for example if I have a short sip, like a snack not a meal, then I might drink several times a month. If I'm injured, then I'll have to drink sooner and in a higher quantity to recover completely."

Shaye looked at him in concern. "Do you need blood now? Your father really caused a lot of injury."

"I had some bagged blood while you slept. It works fine; it just takes more to do the job than fresh blood when I am injured. I have a few more bags downstairs that should last me for a while."

"Fresh blood would help you heal quicker?" she questioned.

"Yes."

"Why didn't you go out to get some, then?"

Rolfston paused. He wanted to find the right words to explain how he was feeling about finding a live donor. He didn't want to pressure Shaye or make her feel like she had to offer herself. However, he did not want to start his mating by lying to his other half.

"It's a complicated feeling. I did not want to leave you alone while you were sleeping and recovering. Now that I know you are my mate, it felt like a betrayal to go out and find a live donor."

"Why? Do you have sex with them?" she asked. Shaye felt jealously, which was ridiculous. She had no right to make any demands of him. They had just met and even though he had accepted that they were mates, she had not fully embraced the idea.

"In the past, I did occasionally. I do not have to be intimate with them, but I do release pheromones to make it pleasurable for them. They often find...release, even if we are not having intercourse. My father enjoys hunting down donors and since he deliberately doesn't release any pheromones, all they feel is terror and pain. I will not put someone through that when I can make it enjoyable instead. I have enough bagged blood for now and can order more later. It will all be fine."

Shaye took a bite of her pizza since she was starving. As she chewed, she thought it over. "Can't you drink from me?"

Rolfston was startled and began choking on his water. "Yes. I could, but because you are my mate, I think the pheromones would get out of control and it would lead to sex. I don't want to push you into the physical relationship yet. I don't know that I would be able to stop myself from claiming you if I was inside you. I don't want to rush you and have you regret choosing me."

"I feel like there is a lot I don't know, things that I need to know to make any kind of decision."

"How about we finish eating first? We can go out to the living room, sit on the couch, and you can ask me any questions you want. I'll answer all of them."

"Okay."

Finishing the pizza, Shaye and Rolfston cleaned up the plates and washed the few dishes. It felt very domestic, he mused. He had grown weary and despaired that he would not find his mate. Many paranormals didn't find their other halves. Sitting on the couch, he turned sideways so that he could see Shaye's face better. It was so expressive, her gray eyes darkening or lightening with her mood. It was fascinating to watch.

"Ask me anything you want," he encouraged her as she turned to face him too.

"How old are you?"

"Two hundred and four years old. How old are you?"

"Thirty. What is your favorite color?"

"Yellow. It's cheery. And yours?"

"Blue. I like all different shades, but a dark blue is my favorite. Although an icy blue, like a Husky's eyes, may be my new favorite," she teased. His eyes really did have that bright icy blue of a husky dog.

"Don't tell my friend Sam that." He laughed. "He'll never let me live it down."

"Why would he tease you about that?"

"He's a werewolf—" he began.

"Wait, what?" she interrupted. "Those are real too?"

"Yes, although they are different from the popular werewolf movies. He is coming over tomorrow with the rest of your things."

"So what all exists? All of the myths?" she asked, a tad hysterical. Werewolves were real and she was going to meet one tomorrow. Of course she was.

"I'll go over the ones that I know exist. Some are so reclusive that they are only myths, so I can't confirm if they really exist or not.

"We'll start with Werewolves. They don't need the full moon to change. It does cause them to be more hyper. I compare Sam on a full moon to a toddler who ate a bowlful of sugar and then drank a couple of espressos. He really can't sit still and just has all this extra energy. They tend to run hungrier at the full moon; my guess is all that extra energy burns a lot of calories. Sam normally goes on a run and tries to keep busy. If there is a Pack, they tend to gather and run and play together in wolf form. Werewolves are faster, have more strength, better hearing and sight than a human would. Wolfsbane can kill them, but it's a poison that can kill most things. They do have a slight allergy to silver for some reason, but it's an irritation and not life-threatening. They'll get some hives and some itching. Werewolves are not immortal, but do live a very long time, about the same as vampires.

"Next, we'll go on to Witches. A version of witches does exist, but they're not really like the ones that Hollywood portrays. They are magic users who live a little longer than most humans, about two hundred years old. They don't need a wand to do their magic, it's just a part of them. They can gather some from the universe around them, but you must be born with magic to be a witch. They mostly use spells but will sometimes make potions as well.

"There are several different types of shapeshifters that I know of. I've met a few different kinds besides the werewolves, but some are so rare I haven't known anyone who has met one. Each one has their own life-span, generally between two and three thousand years old. Although there are rumors that there are some who are immortal. Some shifters change into animals you would know, like wolves or falcons. Some of the rarer ones are supposedly griffins, dragons, and what you would think fairy-tale characters might be, but those also are ones that most paranormals haven't seen.

"The Fae really don't look like they are portrayed in the movies. They usually don't have wings or even pointed ears, but I have met a few that do. They use magic and contrary to popular belief, not all the Fae are gorgeous. They're just like any race; some have more of the Fae/fairy traits you would think of, and some don't. They are immortal though."

Shaye sat there. Had she met any paranormals before and just didn't even realize it? It was crazy to think that there was a whole other world within the one that she knew.

'I bet you have met some,' Rolf answered her. *'We're not that uncommon. You still need to rest though, so how would you feel about just hanging out on the couch and watching a movie?'*

'That sounds good,' she replied. She could let her brain rest for a bit and get used to all the new knowledge.

4

S haye woke up around seven. The sun was already up, and it seemed like Rolf was too. She could hear murmurs coming from the living room, so she got dressed and readied herself to meet a werewolf. She really wanted to like Sam, he had been Rolfston's best friend for a long time.

"Good morning, love. I have coffee if you would like some. Sam brought some donuts and danishes for breakfast too."

"Hi, Shaye. I'm Sam. It's really nice to meet you. I can't tell you how happy I am that Rolf found his mate." Sam walked over to her and held out his hand. He was almost as tall as Rolf, just over six feet. He had longer sun-bleached blond hair, hanging loose over his ears. His eyes were a nice green and looked a little mischievous. He was a broader in the shoulders and had bulkier muscles than Rolf. He looked friendly though and she got a good vibe from him.

"Thank you. It's nice to meet you too," she replied, shaking his hand. Definitely good vibes. He had a light and friendly feel to him, almost like what she would think family would feel like. Which made sense with how close her mate and he were.

"Rolf and I already ate, so we were going to get started with bringing in some of the heavier items first, if that's okay?" Sam asked.

"That is awesome, thank you. You picked out a great assortment of donuts. All of these are my favorites," she grinned.

By the time she was finished eating her donut (or three, don't judge it was a stressful couple of days and she craved sugar when she was stressed) the two guys had already added three new pieces of furniture to her bedroom. There was an oversized chair next to an antique bookcase and a long dresser. Rolf was adding her books to the bookcase, but she didn't see Sam.

Rolfston came over to her. "Are these okay? When we started bonding, I got glimpses of things you liked and thought these were pretty similar." She pulled his head down to hers and gave him a kiss. He had managed to pick out everything she had wanted and placed it in this house. When the kiss was over, she noticed boxes and bags of what looked like clothing next to her suitcases.

"I thought you would want some more things," he told her. "Since you don't have to travel anymore."

Unpacking all the clothes, she saw that they were better quality than what she would normally buy, in her size, and in colors she preferred. He was simply amazing.

"I enjoy surprising you," he said.

"You're going to spoil me," she warned.

"That is the idea."

There was so much to take in—the furniture, clothes, even her few paintings and photographs hung on the wall.

"I wanted it to be the home you have always wanted," he confessed.

"It is. You're wonderful," she said as she pulled him down for another kiss. His lips were amazing and she could spend hours just kissing him.

She turned toward the door when she heard fake coughing.

"Ahem. Innocent eyes over here," Sam teased.

"Uh huh. Somehow, I don't think those eyes have been innocent for a very long time," Shaye teased back.

Sam laughed. "Yup. I'm getting hungry and was going to grab some lunch. Is there anything you guys want?"

After deciding on gyros for lunch, Sam went into town to pick them up. Shaye started putting the clothes away.

"What did you think of Sam?" Rolfston questioned anxiously.

"I like him. He has a good vibe to him," Shaye responded honestly. "You were right. I had nothing to be nervous about."

After Sam returned bearing "gifts of sustenance," they all ate outside on the back patio. It was a gorgeous setting with the porch spanning the length of the house. It was wide enough to have an outdoor table and chair set, a few lounge chairs, and a chimera. The porch led down to a stone paver patio that had its own stone outdoor fireplace. She could see really enjoying the outdoor area when the nights got cooler.

Later that night after Sam left, Shaye turned to him. "Rolf, can I ask you more questions? We never finished last night."

"Anything, anytime."

"How do you turn someone? Will I be your Mate as soon as you turn me? Will I have to drink blood too? Will we have to drink from other people? I don't want to have sex with other people, and I would want us to be monogamous. You mentioned vampires get healing and stuff when they become vampires, but your mother has visions. Did she have that before? Do you have more friends here that I will meet? What are they? Is that rude to ask? Does turning hurt? How long does it take? What does being a mate mean? Is mate with a big 'M' or a little 'm'? Can vampires have kids?" Shaye nervously babbled and basically spewed questions at poor Rolf. She had them pent up in her mind since yesterday and it seemed like now she couldn't turn it off. Way to end on kids when you aren't even his mate yet, she thought to herself.

Rolf looked taken aback. "Whoa. Alright, let me try to work through that.

"You can bite someone, feed from them and not turn them. You have to will it into being as you feed from them. You pass on a special enzyme or something through your fangs. If you decide to turn, then yes, you would need to drink blood too, both to complete the turn and to get nourishment as a vampire. It's not the same as tasting blood when you are human. It tastes like a fine meal, smooth and rich, subtle and vibrant. It's really hard to describe. My mother had what she would call instincts and sometimes prophetic dreams when she was human. They turned into visions after she was turned.

"I have several more friends for you to meet, although not all of them are close by now. Some paranormals are very private and would find asking them what species they are to be rude. I will always tell you and you can always ask along our mental connection. I will make the bite when I turn you enjoyable. You will sleep after I bite you and when you wake up you will have turned. I don't remember it hurting, but I'll check for you. Turning normally takes one to four days, depending on the person, their health, and their gifts. Vampires and humans can have kids, although not all of those children will be able to become a vampire. Two vampires can have children, although it is a rare event. Most of the longer-lived paranormals don't seem to have children easily, although witches don't seem to have the same problem.

"You are my Mate. There will not be another person that I will want to be intimate with. We are monogamous with our mates. You will have to drink, but I can teach you. You can also drink from me or there is bagged blood as well. Mates are similar to human soul mates. 'You complete me,'" he quoted from a movie. "Mates are life-long partners, our other half. We have a mental and physical connection. You are my Mate now; we just haven't completed the mating. Just talking about general mates, it is with a little 'm.' When I address you as my Mate, it's like a title, and it is with a big 'M.'"

"Would my powers get worse?" Shaye wondered fearfully.

"I don't know," he answered. "I know that sucks as an answer, but I will not lie to you. They could get better, as most people have some type of shield after being turned. But there is a chance that your powers could get stronger. One of my gifts is a shield and I think I could help shield you from people's emotions once we have completed the mating. I just don't know for sure."

"Is it okay that I want to wait and think it over? I barely hang on some days, and if it could get worse, I really want to think about it. I do want to be your Mate though, so I'm sorry about making you wait," Shaye replied guiltily.

"I'll wait as long as you need. We can still complete the mate bond without turning you though, if you want to take that step sooner."

"How does that work?"

"Mating is a mental and physical bond. It involves us having an intimate relationship and making a vow to each other through our mental connection during sex. I don't have to bite you to establish the mate bond, only to turn you."

"What about the mate bond? How does that affect you? What if I die or I don't turn, will that hurt you? Will you die too?"

"The mate bond will be stronger after we complete it. We may be able to sense how the other is feeling, maybe share in each other's powers. It varies with each couple. If you would die, I would be heartbroken. If one of us would die, the other would still live. Our lifespans are not linked together that way. Some species are, but not vampires. If we would mate, you would receive a longer lifespan; but unless you turn, you would not have the strengths or weaknesses of a vampire."

"Good. I would not want to be the cause of your dying. Can we wait a little bit and get to know each other better before we mate?" One part of her was thinking she was crazy for even thinking about tying herself to a virtual stranger. The other part of her just knew that he was it, that this was where she was supposed to be. It would appease her questioning side at least a little bit if she waited just a little longer. She had never been one to jump into relationships, especially the physical side of things. Her gift also made that difficult at times.

"I'll wait as long as you need," he repeated. He took her hand in his and kissed her knuckles. He really was content to know she was his Mate. She was a beautiful person, inside and out. "How about we go into town tomorrow and walk around? We can have our first date."

"I would love that."

The next morning was bright with puffy white clouds floating lazily in the sky. The forecast looked perfect for being outside. Shaye got ready for the day, excited to see what Rolf had planned. When she got downstairs, she could hear him in the kitchen.

"Morning, love. I have a travel mug of coffee for you," he said, handing it over to her. "I was thinking we could stop at the bakery in town to grab something for breakfast."

"Did you already drink? Are you all caught up, or do you need more blood before we leave?"

"I feel great. I've healed all the way," he reassured her. "Did you want to drive into town or walk down?"

"Let's walk, it looks like a gorgeous day."

It was still early enough that the streets were not very crowded. They grabbed some pastries at the bakery, the smell of baking sugar heavy in the air. Walking down to the park, they sat under a tree to enjoy their treats. Brushing off his hands, Rolfston stood and held out a hand to help Shaye up.

"I have a surprise for you."

She allowed him to help her up and followed him to the small amusement park area of the park. It was still too early for it to be open, so she wasn't sure why they were walking over there. Rolf walked right up to the carousel and sent a text message. A minute later, a man came over from the ticket booth.

"Sorry," he said. "I had to get the power turned back on." He opened the gate and let them into the carousel area. "Go ahead and pick your favorite steed, I'm going to get the ride turned on."

"We have the whole carousel to ourselves for an hour, if we want it," Rolfston told her.

"This is amazing, thank you! I love old carousels."

"How do you know this is an old one?" Rolf asked,

curious. He had no idea what the difference in carousels were. He just thought she would like it and he knew someone who was willing to help set this up.

"There are a couple of ways to tell. The ears are pointed up. That was the original design until people used them to help climb up onto the horse and the ears started breaking. To solve that problem, they started making the ears folded down, lying against the head. The side of the horse facing the inside of the ride isn't as decorated as the side that faces the outside; it was a money-saving tactic. These also seem like wooden horses; the new ones are made from fiberglass."

"Huh, okay then. How do you know all this?"

Shaye laughed. "I worked in New York for a little bit. There was an amazing carousel museum that I visited one day. I love finding quirky places to visit or things to see."

"That sounds fun. I think it would be fun finding those types of places. Maybe we'll have to plan a trip soon."

Shaye leaned over and gave him a kiss. "Sounds like a plan."

Rolf watched as Shaye climbed up onto one of the horses that moved. He really was a lucky man; Fate had given him the perfect mate. She was compassionate and intelligent; she was caring and strong. He had always loved brunettes and her gray eyes were so unique. Her long wavy hair called him to wrap his fingers in it. Her V-neck dark blue shirt clung to her pert breasts. Those dark blue jeans were molded to her round ass and thighs. No thigh gap there, he thought to himself happily. He couldn't wait until he could feel them wrapped around him.

"Ahem. Are you enjoying the show?" Shaye scolded teasingly, looking back at him.

"You're beautiful, love. Everything about you is gorgeous."

"Thank you," she replied softly. She could feel herself blushing.

They rode the carousel for the hour, trying out the different animals, both the stationary ones and the ones that moved. After wandering around the park and feeding the ducks some food, Rolf asked if she was ready for lunch. "I thought we could go peak in on Sam. He owns a local brewery and does a pretty good lunch menu."

"That sounds good. Does he have burgers? I'm really in the mood for a nice burger."

"He has several," he assured her. "It's not too far away."

He led her to a great old brick building with lots of character. The front doors were large wooden monstrosities with metal bars and accents. The inside was cozy with a wood fireplace, gas wall sconces, wooden tables and chairs, some comfortable-looking booths, and even a few leather couches near a corner fireplace. This was a great place to hang out.

"Outside has a few games like cornhole toss, horseshoes, a chalk drawing area for the kids." Rolf added.

"Rolf! Shaye!" an excited voice yelled out. Turning, they saw Sam waving behind the bar. He walked over to them and asked, "What are you guys doing here?"

"We were looking for a great lunch place and thought yours would be good enough," Rolf teased him.

Sam smacked Rolf upside the head. "You know I have the best fries. Stop giving Shaye ideas."

She laughed at them. "It smells amazing in here and I love the layout. I could totally see just hanging out by the fireplace when it's cold."

Sam led them over to his "favorite" booth. They could

see out over the room. "Do you guys want a menu, or do you want to be surprised?"

"Surprise me, please," Shaye answered. "Could I get a coffee too?"

"Didn't you just finish your coffee?" Rolf asked, surprised.

"There is never enough coffee," she responded seriously.

"Amen to that." Sam laughed as he brought her a large mug, a carafe of coffee, and milk and sugar. He stayed a few minutes to chat with them. They had arrived a littler earlier than the lunch rush. "Let me go grab your food," he left as he heard a bell ding.

Coming back, Sam placed large plates filled with thick burgers, golden brown fries on her plate, crunchy onion rings on Rolf's plate, and small side salads. Shaye took a bite of her burger and fell in love. It was done medium, nice and moist, the lettuce crisp, the tomato slice perfectly ripe, the cheese melty, and the small fried onion crumbles added a great texture. It even had the mix of ketchup and mayo that she loved on a burger. When she bit into the fry, it was crisp on the outside and soft on the inside, perfectly seasoned. "Sam, this is delicious!"

"Thank you. Enjoy your date; it looks like the lunch crowd is starting to come in, so I'm going to have to get going."

Shaye and Rolf ate their lunch. They talked about small things, nothing too heavy. It didn't feel quite like a first date, she thought to herself. They already knew so much about each other that there wasn't any of the awkward pauses or "what-ifs" running through her mind. It was fun just relaxing and enjoying his company. She learned he had a dry sense of humor and loved documentaries. His favorite ice cream was Neapolitan, the weirdo. He claimed it was because he got to eat all the main flavors in one bowl.

She could get behind the chocolate, she had a major chocolate sweet tooth after all. She would rather have a nice piece of chocolate though, maybe a dark chocolate turtle. Yum.

After they finished eating, Rolf dropped some money on the table and held out a hand for her.

"We need to sneak out before Sam sees the money. He won't let me pay otherwise. I was thinking that we could continue walking through town, if you wanted? There are some neat stores if you haven't been there yet."

Since her visit the other day got interrupted, she was excited to see the town. They headed out the door, missing Sam, and headed into town. The main street was lined with all kinds of shops, most of them independent stores. Stopping in front of a pottery store, she looked in the front display window. "Those look like the ones at Sam's. Do you mind if we stop in? I would love to get some for the house."

Rolf was absolutely pleased that she was acting like it was her house now. He had been worried that she wouldn't feel comfortable yet. If she wanted to decorate or add her own touches, he was going to encourage it. "He got them here," he replied. "This is one of our friends' shops. Let's go see if he is in. If you don't see something you like, he does custom orders for his friends too. He's really talented. Oh, and he's Fae."

Well, she did want to meet more of his friends. It felt like her brain was on a bit of an overload though. Just a couple of days ago, she had no idea that paranormals really existed. And it seemed like the myths and legends of each group weren't exactly right either, so she had a lot to catch up on.

"Berkley?" Rolfston called out as he pulled open the store's door.

As Shaye stepped over the threshold, she could feel

the air shiver over her. It was an odd sensation. "Rolf," she whispered urgently. "What was that?"

"Those are my wards to keep evil out," a gorgeous man answered as he came from the back room. "You must be sensitive to feel that. Ah, no, an empath," he corrected as he shook her hand. "I'm Berkley. It's very nice to meet Rolfston's Mate.

"I'm Shaye. It's nice to meet you too. I love your coffee mugs." She responded while trying not to stare at him. He had silvery blond hair and these deep bluish-purple eyes. It was a very unique look. He wasn't quite as tall as Rolf was, but still taller than her. He had on tight black jeans, a cream Henley shirt with the sleeves rolled up showing off a leather wrist band on his left arm. He also had on a charcoal-colored apron, but instead of a solid front, it looked like the fabric split down the middle at the waist, with the one side overlapping the other. '*It's a potter's apron*," Rolf told her. '*He must be going to work on some new pieces today.*'

"Hmm, hold on. I have some that I think need to go home with you," Berkley said heading back to the backroom.

'*He likes you, love,*' she heard in her head.

'*How do you know? We only said hi.*'

'*The backroom has his special pieces, the ones not for general sale.*'

Berkley came back out holding a pair of mugs. They were gorgeous with varying shades of blue and swirls of silver. They made her feel peaceful and relaxed holding them.

Berkley made a contented sound. "I knew these would be the right ones. They should help ground you and keep your energy levels steady after a healing. Make sure to drink from them as soon as you can after healing someone, doesn't matter what you drink as long as you use the mugs."

She looked at him questioningly.

"Magic," he said, laughing. "Some of my special pieces have a bit of magic in them. I get the urge to make them and then when I meet someone, I know who they are for."

"Thank you." Shaye was touched. Rolf had such good friends.

She noticed Berkley studying Rolf. "Rolf can use them too. They're safe for his drink and will help him feel better. What happened man? Your energy looks like it was recently damaged. Badly."

"My father paid a little visit a few days ago. Shaye found me and interrupted him and managed to get me healed. Mom reinforced the wards while Shaye was recovering. I had some bagged blood on hand, so I was able to drink without leaving the house. I may need to adjust the wards; they let him in because he was with me, but it didn't differentiate between me being willing to have him there and him dragging me home unconscious. Do you have time later to come over and see what you think would be helpful?"

"Definitely. Does tomorrow after closing work? I can bring a few things that may help. If he's reached this stage of aggression, then we can put a strong ward in place to keep out any evil, similar to what is on the store. We can extend it to the house grounds too, just to be safe."

"That would be great. I want it safer for Shaye," Rolf responded.

"And you," Shaye added.

After Berkley refused any payment, saying the mugs were a Mating Gift, the couple left the store and wandered down to the bookstore. It was another building that she fell in love with. There were cozy window seats and couches scattered throughout the store. A cute café sat in the front corner as well and she grabbed some more coffee and paid for a couple of books she found.

"Should I be worried about your coffee consumption?" Rolf laughed.

"Nope. As long as I get my coffee, no one gets hurt," she joked back.

"I have one more stop to make," Rolfston said, stopping by a medical building.

"Are you feeling alright?" Shaye asked, alarmed.

"I'm fine. I just have to put an order in."

An order? What? As she stood there, Shaye realized that this town must know of the paranormal creatures who lived here. Why else would the doctor's office take a blood delivery order? He didn't even specify which blood type to the receptionist, so clearly it wasn't for a medical issue.

A man suddenly stuck his head out of a door down the hallway. "Good afternoon, Rolfston. Is this a rush order or can it wait a little bit? I don't have any extra available right now."

"It can wait. I have a little left at home, but may need more in a month or so." Rolf responded.

'The doctor here is paranormal. I'm not even sure what kind he is, but he has been here forever,' Rolf explained to Shaye.

"Doc, you got a minute?"

The doctor looked down at his watch. "I have about five minutes until my next patient," he said, coming out of the room.

"Doc, this is my Shaye," Rolf said proudly. "Shaye, this is Doctor Theodoropoulos. Everyone just calls him Dr. T or Doc," Rolf introduced her to the white-haired man. He didn't look old, maybe around forty-five. Definitely not old enough to have the bright white hair. He had the darkest eyes, either a really dark brown or black.

"Nice to meet you," they both said.

The door to the clinic opened with Doc's next patient. "Just give me a few hours' notice when you need that, Rolf. I'll wait to refill until I hear from you."

'Doc has had white hair for as long as I have known him. I think it's his natural color, not age. His clinic helps treat the local para group, as well as the humans that live in town. This town has become something of a haven for our kind. Even a lot of the humans here know about us, mostly the ones that have had family here for a few generations. It's been great not having to leave and set up a new identity and home.' Rolf said as they walked out of the clinic.

'Did you have to do that a lot?' She didn't even think about the aging problem and dealing with strangers.

'Until I moved here, I did. You could get maybe thirty years or so before people started noticing you didn't age like they did. We do age, it's just extremely slowly. Vampires can live to be around two thousand years from what I've learned. Werewolves can live to around fifteen hundred to two thousand years, witches to about two hundred years, and Fae are the only ones I know of that are immortal. I'm not sure on some of the other shifter types, as they are extremely secretive of their abilities.'

Shaye thought about that as they walked down the street. That was a long time to live, especially if she would have to keep saying goodbye to her friends. She would have Rolfston by her side at least, and the town with some of the other paranormals. Even then though, some of them would pass on before them. It seemed like a very lonely life he had led until he found this town and he could settle down some roots.

5

There was annoying knocking on the front door as they were about to sit down to eat dinner.

Rolf sighed. "That's Berkley. He's the only one annoying enough to knock like that. He thinks it's funny." He gave his dinner a forlorn look and went to let his friend in.

Shaye just shook her head at the two of them. For being two hundred-ish years old and however old Berkley was, they certainly acted like kids sometimes. She got up and made another plate of dinner and set another place setting.

"Tea, coffee, water, or soda?" She shouted out the kitchen door.

"Water would be great," Berkley answered as he came in. "It smells delicious in here."

"I already made you a plate, so go ahead and sit down. We're having zucchini lasagna with a side salad."

The friends ribbed each other over dinner but made sure to include Shaye in their conversation. It was nice to make more friends from town. Before yesterday, the only other long interaction had been with her supervisor at the hospital.

"When do you start work, Shaye?" Berkley asked.

She checked her watch. Her internal calendar had been off since she had slept so long after healing Rolf. "Woah, Monday actually. I'll have to get my work stuff together this weekend. I already met with my supervisor and got my hospital ID, so as long as I can find where my work clothes ended up, I'll be good to start."

"Are you sure you will be okay to start?" Rolf asked, concerned. It hadn't been that long since she had worn herself to the point that her body had begun to shut down.

"I'll meditate before I start work and get my shields back to normal. Plus, I have Berkley's special coffee mugs now," she said, smiling at him. "It will be good to get back into a routine."

After dinner was cleaned up, they went to sit in the living room. Berkley claimed the recliner and Shaye curled up next to Rolfston on the couch. For a few minutes, they all just relaxed and let their dinner settle.

"Thank you for dinner, Shaye. That was delicious," Berkley complimented.

"You're welcome anytime," she offered.

"Well…not any time," Rolf responded as he teasingly kissed and nibbled along her neck.

Berkley just laughed at them. "Righto, I'll make sure to call first maybe."

He got up to stretch. "Did you want to go over where the property lines are and set the wards, Rolf? I can ward anything that belongs to you, so the house, gate, and the rest of the estate. If you have a map of it, then we won't have to walk the whole property to set the lines and can get it done before it's too dark out. I think if we work together, between our two magics we should be able to make the estate secure. I can place a few runes at the doorways and windows of the house for added security."

"How big is the property? I haven't really explored it," she asked. She saw the front of the house with its long, gated driveway. It really was set back a nice distance from the road, but still maintained a clear line of sight down the driveway.

Rolf stood up as well. "Let's go on the back porch and I can show you a little bit more. I didn't get to show you all of that area back there yet. The backyard has the porch and patio area with about an acre of cleared ground. I just put in the outdoor fireplace and the patio last year. It's a nice space to hang out when it's not too humid. I am planning on putting in a vegetable garden or a small greenhouse too, but haven't gotten around to it yet," he added as he opened the back door and turned on the outdoor lights. The sun was starting to set, coloring the sky with pinks and oranges.

Shaye looked around. She could totally see enjoying this space with friends. Maybe they should get a grill and start having some BBQ's.

'I love that idea,' Rolf told her. 'I've been meaning to get some hammocks here too. Sam introduced me to the hammock at his apartment, but I haven't figured out where they should go here yet.'

'What about by the end of the patio, near the tree line? You could put up four posts, crossbeams in the middle, making a hammock pavilion? You could fit four that way, maybe a hammock chair or small firepit in the middle. The trees would provide some shade, or we could add some shade sails.'

'I love it. I'll call the contractor I used for the porch and get it started,' Rolf said excitedly.

"What are you two talking about?" Berkley asked.

"Putting up a hammock stand," Rolf answered.

"Oooh! I will totally be over here all the time. Sam

told me I was stealing his hammock too much, so I'm limited to twice a week now. I don't have room for one in the apartment over the shop," Berkley pouted.

"Well, we may put up several, so there should be room for you." Rolfston rolled his eyes. "Anyway, Shaye. The property goes a bit farther out toward the sides and back. I own a little bit of the forest area, which is popular with some of the local shifters like Sam. I let them run here when they need to shift, and it helps keep the not-in-the-know humans away. There is fencing around most of the property to help keep everyone safe. There is a small pond further back on the property too. If you go straight back, you will also end up in the National Park. The shifters like being able to have that little bit of protection from hunters as well." Rolf pointed out where the different features were located.

Berkley snorted. "A little bit of the forest, ha."

Shaye looked over at him, eyebrow raised.

"He's being modest. The house sits on about seventy acres, most of it wooded. He calls it a house; I call it an estate."

"It's not an estate, it's just my house and some land. I like being able to have safe land that my friends can come over to shift and run when they need to. Or come work magic," Rolf protested. He turned back to Shaye. "I have a few walking paths that I've worn down through the woods. We can explore it more tomorrow when it isn't getting dark, but if you decide to explore on your own later, just don't go past the fencing and you should be safe after we get these wards up tonight."

They headed back inside the house and Rolf grabbed the property survey map from his office. "This one should be up to date. I had it made a few years ago."

Shaye watched as Berkley set a few crystals around the map. Rolf put his hand on Berkley's shoulder, and

Berkley began tracing the edges of the property line while saying what might have been a spell. She couldn't understand the language he was using. They traced the lines a few times and when it flashed bright white, they stopped.

"Okay, that should take care of the property. Rolf, are you okay with me adding the runes around the doors and windows? I don't have to make them big, but I will have to mark the frames," Berkley clarified.

"That's fine, I don't mind. I would much rather the house be secure. Plus, I think they look pretty neat."

Shaye watched as Berkley went to each door and window and traced words on the frames. Once he uttered a few words, they blazed bright white like the map had. It took him about an hour to get it completed, but when he was done Shaye could feel the difference. It gave the house a peaceful, calm feeling, like when you got a snuggle hug from a loved one.

Berkley left when he was done, citing the need to get up early for the shop.

It was Sunday night and Shaye and Rolfston were relaxing in the living room reading on the couches. They had spent the day exploring the estate grounds. The pond had so many wildflowers growing near it, that Shaye imagined it was a haven for all kinds of butterflies. She would have to try to find them one day. She was glad Rolf had a fence line, or there was no way she would be able to tell where the property ended. In some spots, the woods would open up into a clearing, and in other spots the woods seemed to just go on forever. She could imagine how beautiful everything must look with a layer of snow coating it in the winter and with fresh blooms in the spring.

"Does the town get much snow?"

Rolf looked up. "We get a pretty good snowfall at least once in the winter. It makes the woods look magical. We usually don't get snowed in though, so not too much snow. What brought that on?"

"I was just thinking the woods would look pretty with a coating of snow. I've lived in places that never got snow, but when I lived in the Northeast, I definitely saw some snow. Not as bad as some of my friends in Canada though."

"I like to send my mom a picture of the first big snow fall. She loves the snow."

"She lives in Europe?"

"Yup, right now she is in England. She likes to move around every ten years or so and tries out the different countries. We grew up near England, so she's comfortable there."

"Does she ever come over here?"

Rolf looked sad. "No, not since my father is here. I go over there about once a year to see her; we talk a lot on the phone, video chat weekly."

"How old is your mom? Did she turn before or after you?" Shaye asked.

Rolf closed his book and put it down on the coffee table. "It's not a pleasant story. I'm definitely not the hero this time."

"Tell me," she encouraged. "I want to know everything about you, including the bad parts. Not that I think you have many," she teased, trying to get a smile out of him.

He sighed. "Short answer, about two or three years after I did. My mother never spoke of my father. I didn't know how they got together, how or why they made me, why he was never there. I wanted a father like everyone else. I worked on the farm with my mom, we made ends meet. Until I turned twenty-five, I had never met him. On my twenty-fifth birthday he snuck up behind me and tore my throat out to change me. My turning was painful, later I found out it was deliberately painful, but at the time I thought it was just how it was.

"Afterward, he was so apologetic, saying it was the only way to make me like him. He wanted to spend time together, he wanted to teach me. He said he would make sure my mom was provided for while I was gone, but I couldn't be near her for a while until I got myself under control. That was not true by the way; my shield helped me with control. However, I thought I wasn't in control because he kept interfering to make me doubt myself. He would slip sleeping potions in my drinks and I would wake up next to someone who had been completely drained. There were bite marks, so of course I thought that I was a monster who had lost control, blacked out, and killed someone.

"I would never want to hurt my mom, so I stayed away longer. I kept hoping that I would stop blacking out and I could go back to see her. I sent money back whenever I had some, so that I knew she would be okay.

"I started noticing some things though. People seemed scared of him. The few vampires I met always submitted to him or avoided him altogether. I heard stories from villagers and vampires alike, whispered hushed stories. Finally, an old woman came to me and told me that she saw my father drug me and drop my unconscious body on the ground. He then lured in a traveler that was passing by and killed them. He made sure to rub their blood on me and to stage it like I had killed them. I was so angry and hurt. I never wanted to kill anyone, and I had been hating myself for not having enough control. I had been working so hard on myself, trying all different things to stay in control of myself, but I kept having these blackouts. Turns out that he had been behind it all along. He wanted to keep control over me.

"When I confronted him, he just laughed at me. Said that I could follow in his footsteps and help him to rule over everyone, or he would destroy me. I asked why? Why would he do that? He told me that this plan had been years in the making. He had heard rumors, legends. Legends which stated that if a vampire breeds with a human, and they are changed on their twenty-fifth birthday, there will be the chance of them either dying, remaining human, or turning with additional powers. Well, I had survived so he wanted his due for all the work of having to take time out of his life to breed someone and then come back for it…me. It turns out my mother never spoke of him because she was raped by him. She never wanted me to know, never wanted me to know the pain she went through. Her family helped her buy the farm in a different town as a "widow" so that she could raise me on her own without being an outcast. My grandparents came with her and lived with us until they died when I was fifteen. We had enough money to hire one farmhand before I left so that she wasn't left on the farm by herself.

"I decided I was done with his lies and snuck out while he was hunting. I found another vampire group during my travels back to my mother. They knew who he was just by name, but they still took me in for a few months and taught me the correct ways of doing things. Everything he taught me was wrong, he was trying to make me a monster like he was. I didn't have to kill to feed. I didn't have to let them feel terror when I drank. I could control my powers. I was a decent person in my human life, so I could be a decent vampire. Being a vampire didn't make me evil.

"It had been at least two years, maybe closer to three, by the time I got back home. The farm was still there, but I couldn't find my mom. I searched all through the house and then started in the fields. I found our farmhand first. He had been killed. It looked like bite marks. I was panicked, trying to find her. When I finally found her, she was lying on the ground close to death. He had been following me and rushed back before I could get there. He attacked her and left her there but made sure to time it so that I could see her die. He had started to turn her but hadn't given her enough blood to finish the process. What he didn't know, was that the vampires I spent time with had told me how to turn someone. I gave her some of my blood and she pulled through, but she is now always a little weaker than other vampires because of the way she was turned. She doesn't blame me, but I do. If I hadn't left, if I hadn't just blindly accepted his lies of wanting to be my father, that never would have happened to her."

Shaye climbed into his lap and gave him a hug. "Now you listen to me. Vlad is at fault, no one else. He assaulted your mother both times. He turned you without consent. You must have felt overwhelmed and like he was a lifeline in a new strange world. He lied to you. When you found out what he was doing, you left. You found others and got more informed. You saved your mother. The only thing you are guilty of, is thinking the best of him." She gave him a soft kiss. "How old is your father? Do you know?"

"Old. That's part of the reason people were afraid of him. He's one of the oldest still around. It's rare that anyone from that generation reached anywhere close to two thousand years old. There was so much fighting and war when he was turned, that many of them didn't make it past five hundred, much less to a thousand. Add in that he's just plain evil, and no one wants to cross him. My best guess based on what I heard, is that he is probably around fifteen hundred. Maybe seventeen hundred. The stories I've heard is that he kills anyone that could be stronger than him and anyone who is close to his age is killed too. He managed to get a few followers through the years. I stay here to help keep him away from this area. I have a few friends scattered around that keep an ear out for him too."

Rolf hugged her closer and just held her for a few minutes. "Thank you for listening, love." He bent to give her a soft kiss.

6

It was Saturday morning and Shaye was really enjoying sleeping in. Her shifts at the hospital started early and she was still adjusting to the schedule, even after a week. Unfortunately, she could hear her phone beeping insistently with text notifications. She sighed and rolled over, hoping to not wake up Rolfston.

"Crap!" she shouted.

"What? What's wrong?" Rolf sat up. He had a bad case of bedhead and looked very bleary-eyed this early in the morning.

"My friend Tess is coming. She said she'll be here in an hour or so."

"Is that bad? Were you expecting her? She could stay here, if you wanted."

"It's not bad, per se. I was not expecting her, which means she has a reason for finding me. Not that I was hiding from her, but you know what I mean. She gets dreams sometimes, which are normally prophetic, so she must have seen something. We've been friends a long time. I met her while I was at college. Tess was already out of school, she's a few years older than me, and she had found a job in New Orleans. We just really clicked and became really good friends. She would hang out with Ian and me. Ian is my oldest friend; I've known him since high school and we went to the same college together. Both of them have always been there for me, dropped what they were doing to come help me," Shaye explained as she ran into the bathroom to get ready.

An hour later, a car pulled up to the gates and Shaye's phone rang.

"Let me in, heifer. And tell your boy toy to have the wards let me through." Shaye could hear the laughter in her friend's voice, so hopefully nothing was wrong.

"I'm coming—"

"Well, stop that and let me in!"

"Are you twelve?" Shaye asked. "The gates are opening, come on in."

Shaye and Rolf were waiting on the porch by the time her friend had made it up the driveway. Shaye felt Rolf tense as the short blonde with a pixie bob cut got out of the car. "What's wrong?" she asked him. He just shook his head.

"Greetings, Vampire," Tess stated. "Thanks for letting me in."

"Good morning, Witch," Rolf responded. "All of Shaye's friends are welcome," he added. Tess's hazel eyes were not very friendly at the moment and he wasn't sure what he could have done to upset her.

"We're family, not just friends. I adopted her long before you knew her."

"Tess! What has gotten into you? And why did you call her a witch?" she asked, turning to Rolf.

Rolfston looked at Shaye, then Tess, and back again at Shaye. "Uh uh. Nope. No. Not going there. I'll let her explain. You can be mad at her, not me."

Shaye opened the front door. "I'm getting some coffee.

I want both of you in the living room and I want to know what is going on." She stomped inside. She was going to need a lot of coffee for today.

After taking several sips of her drink, she let out a long sigh. "So, the crazy train is apparently still running strong around here. What was that all about?"

Rolf shook his head again and pointed at Tess. Clearly, he didn't want to cause any problems this morning. Had Shaye not known her friend was a witch? Why wouldn't Tess have told her, he thought to himself.

Tess looked down at her hands. "I may have left out a few facts about myself," she said. "I am a witch. My family have always been witches. Most of us, I mean my family not all witches, are down south. My mom's family are in North Carolina and my dad's are in Louisiana and Texas. I was visiting family when you came into town and I felt drawn to you. I knew we would be friends, so I stayed there and found a job. I'm seventy-five years old, so I look pretty good for my age, right?" she tried joking.

"Why wouldn't you tell me? I told you all about me, about my gifts and my family. I would have kept your secret," Shaye replied, hurt. Tess was one of her oldest (quite possibly literally now) friends.

"I couldn't. My family doesn't allow us to tell outsiders, people who don't know about the paranormal, about our magic. I finally had a dream about you being here with your vampire and it showed us talking about this. I figured if you already knew the paranormal existed, then I wasn't really breaking the family rules and could finally tell you the truth. The dreams also showed a dark cloud coming over the area in the future. I don't know how soon the danger will be here, but I wanted to come and warn you."

Shaye sat there for a minute. She was still hurt, but she also hid her gifts from people at first, so she could understand where Tess was coming from. Tess had always been there for her, not matter what time of day or how far away she was. The truth was that while she had hidden something, she had also proven with her actions that she was a real friend.

"Can you forgive me?" Tess asked, her hazel eyes shiny with tears.

"Yes, but you have to be nicer to Rolf, he's my Mate. And no more secrets, okay?" Shaye added, hugging her friend.

"Deal. Your vampire is rather pretty to look at," Tess whispered.

"Just wait until you meet the rest of his friends, they're all good-looking," Shaye confessed.

Rolf just shook his head and headed into the kitchen to make some eggs for breakfast. He thought they had some bacon in the fridge as well, so he could make a quick meal. He wanted to give them a few minutes to catch up without him standing there. He thought Tess would be more comfortable that way. He smiled to himself as he heard them laughing in the other room. It would be good to have additional paranormals around Shaye in case his father came back. That had to be what the "dark cloud" was that Tess mentioned. If she had any more premonitions, it could only help them prepare, he thought.

"Just how many of these friends are single?" Tess asked after Rolf left.

Shaye laughed. "So far, the two I have met are both single and gorgeous, although in different ways."

"I cannot wait to meet them. I am going to grab some coffee. Did you want more?" Tess asked, grabbing Shaye's empty cup.

Rolf heard a throat clearing from the doorway as he

bent down to put the bacon in the oven. Looking up, he saw Tess standing in the doorway.

"I wanted to apologize for my entrance. I didn't realize you were mates, I thought you were just dating. She has had some crappy dating experiences and I was being a little overprotective. I made assumptions and didn't use my magic to look harder at your connection. I have always hoped that one day she would find a forever person. I'm happy she found you," Tess added sincerely.

"Thank you. I'm glad she has had you. It seems like she had a rough time of life and not too many of the people who were supposed to love her did what was right. Are you staying in town for a while? We have extra room, if you wanted to stay here?" Rolf offered, trying to figure out how long Tess might stay.

"I would love that, thanks. My job is completely remote, so I was planning on finding a place in town to rent for a while. I planned on moving here if Shaye was staying. I would love to live closer to her again."

"Really? You're going to move here? That would be awesome!" Shaye exclaimed. She bounced over and gave her friend a huge hug.

"I offered for Tess to stay here at the house. We have plenty of rooms, and it would give you a chance to catch up. You can stay as long as you want, no need to rent someplace," he added to Tess.

Tess and Shaye stayed in the kitchen chatting with Rolf while he finished cooking breakfast. After breakfast, Rolf went to work in his office. He wanted to give them more time to catch up and for Tess to be comfortable in the space. Plus, he always had paperwork that he could catch up on.

'Thank you. You are the best mate ever,' he heard Shaye tell him.

Shaye sat across from Tess on the couch. They were

both sitting sideways, facing each other, holding cups of coffee.

"This reminds me of the college days," Shaye remarked.

"It does," Tess snorted. "Some things never change." After taking a bracing sip of her coffee, she took a deep breath. "I really am sorry that I didn't tell you I was a witch sooner. I really wanted to, but the family wouldn't give their permission. If I went against them, there's always the chance, although probably a small one, that I would be outcast. It can be hard to be completely on your own, and I was scared. I don't think they would have; my family isn't really like that. But I have seen it happen to other people, and the fear of that kept me from speaking out. I kept hoping that I could tell you so that I didn't have to ghost you one day. We stop aging in appearance around twenty-five to thirty years old. I'll start aging slowly at around one hundred years old, but not quite at the same pace as a human. If I hadn't been able to tell you the truth, you would have started to notice I wasn't aging the same as you, and I would have had to disappear. That would have sucked." Tess smiled sadly.

"Well, now I know and I can keep you forever," Shaye joked. She did know in the back of her head that she would live longer than Tess if she turned, but today was for happy thoughts only, she decided.

"Rolf didn't tell me a lot about witches, so spill," she demanded.

"Where to start... We live in our family groups, generally huge extended family groups. We tend to mate with other witches, although there have been a few inter-species matings in the past. Witches can recognize our mates in our dreams; usually the dream appears close to when we are going to meet them. We live longer, about two hundred years, but can still get sick just like a regular human. Witches work in magic, but we do not need wands. Sometimes we create potions, but most of the magic is done through spells. The extra things you would think of like crystals and herbs, are only occasionally used for spells that need to be extremely strong or cover large distances, used to amplify, enhance, or enforce the spellwork. Most spells are created simply from the magic we are born with and what exists out there naturally in the world."

Shaye nodded. "What does your family think of you moving here? Do you think they'll be okay with it? Do you think you'll stay here?"

"I missed you. You're like my sister. I knew we would be best friends the moment I met you. My family is great, and one day I'll take you back home and you can see the real craziness that they are since you know all about us now. They won't have to pretend to be on good behavior," she said as she laughed. "I'm meant to be here. The dreams have said so. I think this house and lands will be a grand place for all of us."

"All of us?" Shaye queried.

"I think you have a few more friends here that will be coming over soon. It's big enough to hold a few of us, keep us all together," Tess replied. She wasn't sure how much to say. The future wasn't firm yet, but she saw Rolf opening the doors of his house to all of his friends. It would be a great family to be in and she really wanted to be part of it.

'I've played with that idea for years,' Rolf told Shaye. *'This house is huge for just the two of us. I never said anything before because Sam and Berkley have their places. My friend Gawain travels a lot and never puts down roots. He does stay here when he is town, but I don't know if he would want something more permanent. I also didn't want to form my own Clan and bring down my father's wrath on my friends,'* he added.

'*I think it's a great idea. Even if the guys keep their own places in town, we could offer them rooms here too.*' Shaye loved the idea of her friends gathered together. '*Berkley might come just for the hammocks.*' She laughed.

'*True. Speaking of, the contractors should be starting this week to put the hammock pavilion in. I wanted to have time to enjoy it during the rest of the fall before winter hits. It should only take them a few days. I think most of it is making sure the concrete is set before we use it. I ordered some outdoor hammocks as well.*'

'*That will be fun! We should have everyone over when it's ready; pick up a grill and have a party in the backyard,*' Shaye replied. It would be nice to read out in the hammock area. '*Is it okay to tell Tess about the problem with your father?*'

'*Absolutely. She needs to know why the wards are in place and so that she can be safe when she's off the grounds. She might have some good ideas too.*'

Shaye focused back on Tess. "We would love to have you stay here. You know I always wanted a family. We can make our own. Rolf has some great friends in town, and a few others that live around the world. He said he didn't formally start his own Clan because of his father. It's quite the story and Rolf said it was important for you to know of the danger if you are going to stay here. The wards protect the house and the grounds, but you'll need to be careful when you are out in town. His father is evil," she informed her friend.

"Those are some pretty serious wards around the property, and I felt the additional runes on the front door too. What happened?" Tess asked.

Shaye spent some time explaining how she met her mate. They spent the next several hours talking about the problem and ways they might be able to help protect the house and the town better. Eventually the conversation turned back to Shaye and Rolf.

"So why haven't you mated yet?" Tess asked curiously.

"It just seems so crazy, right? To meet someone and then basically marry them in paranormal terms, all within about two weeks!" Shaye exclaimed.

"I guess it does for humans. We are lucky to know when we meet our mate that they are the perfect partner for us chosen by Fate. Our courtships are usually really short, maybe a couple of days until the mating is completed? What holds you back?" Tess questioned. She wanted the best for her friend and knew that Fate would have found her the perfect mate. Rolf seemed like he loved Shaye. Once she met her own mate, she had no plans of waiting to claim him.

"I don't know. Everything I am used to says it is too fast. I'm not sure about turning either. We don't know if my powers will grow, if they will be easier to control or not. Rolf can shield, so he thinks he can help, but he's not sure. It seems like a lot of unknowns. You know how bad it can get. If my power grows at all, but being able to shield myself doesn't, it would be horrible. I don't want to leave Rolfston alone either, if I wouldn't turn and die of old age. Plus, how is that fair to make him take care of me when I am old?" Shaye vented.

'I will always care for you, love. Young, old. Human or vampire. You are my Mate, my everything.' Rolf told her.

Shaye winced. *'Sorry, I didn't mean to project that so loudly. I do love you. I'm working on the rest.'*

'I told you I will wait for you, there is no rush,' Rolf reassured her.

'I know.'

Tess waited patiently until they were done talking to each other. "If you turn, I do believe that you would get help with your powers. I don't think Fate would make things worse for you when you choose to be with your mate. I can see how it would be scary though," she admitted. "Who do you think will tell you it is too fast? All of your friends here are paranormals and used to how quickly mating happens. Your human friends will accept it because they love you. I think a lot of them have some inkling on the paranormal world anyway; they were pretty quick to accept your gift. You don't have to turn right now, even if you mate," Tess added.

"I know. Rolf told me that too. It just seems mean to not accept all of it at the same time, to make him wait."

'Shaye, I will be happy accepting a long courtship, a quick mating and a turn later, or a turn never. I just want to love you. My Mate,' Rolf added.

Shaye sent him a hug. Well, hopefully it felt like a hug. She hadn't tried sending sensations over their bond before.

"He is your fated mate. He will want what makes you happy. I think Rolf forgot to add something though. If you mate, but do not turn, you will still get his increased lifespan. You will not receive any of the other vampire characteristics though. You would still be more vulnerable to illness and injuries, but your lifespan would lengthen to match his. If you do not complete your mating, then your aging process would still be a human's. Fate really does want mates to be together in whatever way is best for them." Tess told her.

Shaye looked over at her friend. "What about you? When you find your mate?"

"I plan on claiming my mate the day I find him. Life can be too short, and I don't want to waste any time. I know mating will be like any other relationship; just because Fate knows that at our core we are perfect for each other, that doesn't mean that there won't be work and compromise to keep the relationship healthy. I think knowing your mate is meant only for you gives you a head start though. My dad died early from health problems. Witches can get human illnesses like cancer and heart disease, and even magic cannot cure everything. My mom misses him every day, but I know she doesn't regret the time they had together. I want as much time with my mate as possible, so when I meet him, I want to claim him," Tess said softly. "Anyway, what does your heart say? And I hate being that corny, for the record," Tess complained.

"That he's mine. And I'm his. I do love him, even though it's only been a short time. I can see into his thoughts and memories. I know what kind of man he is."

"Then that's all you need to know. The rest you can figure out later," Tess encouraged her.

Taking a deep breath, Shaye got ready for bed. She made sure to shield her thoughts as she got dressed. Tess was right, it was time. Shaye couldn't see her life without Rolf, his kindness, his humor. He was like her best friend and lover all rolled up into one amazing package. Even though Rolf had offered to sleep in his own bedroom, they had already been sharing the same bed every night. They hadn't had sex yet, but she loved sleeping next to him. She trusted him. She still wasn't ready to turn, but she wanted tonight to be her Mating Night. Shaye brushed her hair out from its ponytail, knowing Rolf loved to play with her hair. She put on a black thong that tied at the sides and pale pink corset decorated with black lace and ties. She bought this outfit ages ago because it made her feel a little naughty and a lot sexy, but never had an opportunity to wear it. Rolf was going to love it and she loved that she had a special outfit for their Mating Night.

Rolf was reading in bed, but he quickly put his book down as she came into the room. "Wow, you look amazing," he breathed.

Shaye walked over to straddle him on the bed. "I'm ready. To mate, but not to turn yet. I love you and would love to be your mate."

"Oh, love. You already are my Mate, but I can't wait to make it official." Rolf rubbed his hands down her body, loving the way the corset accentuated her curves. Her gorgeous breasts were pushed up. He ran a finger along the top of the corset where it met her skin, loving the way she shivered. He grabbed her full ass, pulling her toward him and flipping them so that she was on the bottom. Shaye pulled him down for a kiss, her tongue curling around his, rubbing them together. He ran his hands lightly down her sides, teasing at the seams of her lips, grabbing onto her thighs. Rolf spread her legs wider and moved down to lie between her legs. His tongue traced from her ankles to her knees.

Shaye giggled. "Not there, that tickles."

Rolf hummed and moved further up her thighs. "You smell so good, love. I can't wait for a taste." He felt her watching him and used his teeth to untie her underwear. As it fell apart, he leaned in and gave her a teasing lick. Her lips were full and glistening already. He moaned, enjoying the feel and scent of her. Her blood ran close to the surface, enhancing her natural flavors and smell. He would never get enough of this, he thought as he ran his thumbs up the center, spreading her lips to get to the main prize. Her hips lurched toward him as he licked her clit, firmly moving the tip of his tongue in circles over it in the way she liked.

"Oh, Rolf. Yes, just like that. A little harder. Ahh!"

Shaye screamed as he got the pressure just right. He grabbed her hips to hold her still as he ate her out. "Yes, please. I need more. Please, I'm so empty."

Rolf thrust two fingers into her tight, wet heat. Her walls clamped around his fingers as he worked his fingers in and out of her, creating the friction she needed. He couldn't wait until he could feel that wrapped around his dick. He was so fucking hot right now, his face covered in her arousal and his dick leaking precum.

"In me, Rolf. I need you. I want to be your mate."

He pulled his fingers out of her cunt, making sure she saw him lick them clean. She really was delicious, and he couldn't wait for more.

She urged him up, kissing him as he balanced over her, tasting herself on his lips. He always made sure she felt incredible when they were together. He made her fly. She reached down, peeling his boxer briefs low and letting his dick out. He was hard, drops of precum at the tip. Grasping his dick, she stroked him up and down, loving the sounds he made as she twisted her hand when she got to the tip.

Rolf pulled away, kicking off his underwear. *'How do you want this, love?'*

Shaye moved to get on her hands and knees. She loved doggie style, it hit her G-spot just right. Plus, she could keep the corset on. *'Like this?'*

"Hmm, I love this view. Your body is perfect for me, curves, your ass is framed perfectly by the corset, I love your thighs. Fate was so good to me." He moved between her thighs, reaching down to rub her clit one more time. He eased into her tight heat. It was worth every moment of waiting.

Shaye gasped as he filled her. He was so big, she could feel him rubbing against her walls, rubbing against her G-spot. He was warm and filled her completely. He started out slowly thrusting, just a steady slow pace that drove her mad as his dick stretched her opening and created delicious friction against her walls. He reached around and slid a hand into the top of her corset to play with her nipples. She felt an invisible tongue licking against her clit, causing her cunt to get even wetter. She could hear the sounds of their bodies coming together. As the tongue began to press harder on her clit, giving her the friction she needed, Rolf braced an arm against the wall, allowing him to thrust even more deeply into her welcoming body. Her orgasm rushed through her as she felt his teeth bite into her neck.

'I take you, Shaye, as my Mate. To love and cherish forevermore.'

'I take you, Rolfston, as my Mate. To love and cherish forevermore.'

Shaye felt him swallowing against her neck, but all she felt was pleasure. He reached down and rubbed her clit, coaxing another orgasm out of her as he drank. She felt him everywhere; in her body, in her mind, wrapped around her soul. Their bond flared and snapped into place. They were finally, completely mates.

"Rest, love. I'll get you some water," Rolf said as he eased from her body.

She woke up a few moments later when she felt him remove her corset. She just wanted to float, so she simply sent him a questioning sound.

"I didn't think this would be too comfortable to sleep in. I have some water for you. I didn't take much, but the water can't hurt," Rolf said.

Sitting up, she drank her bottle of water and watched her Mate. He was so incredibly sexy. His tall body had sparse body hair, other than at his groin and of course his thick head of black hair. He had a little bit of scruff on his face since it was the end of the day, but he was normally clean shaven. His blue eyes were so bright with love it made her catch her breath. His stomach was a six-pack that she just wanted to pet and his dick...well, that was something dream worthy. Seven inches, thick but not too thick. It hit her in all the right places. She was getting wet again, and by the flare of his nostrils and wide pupils, he could smell it.

She lay back on the bed as he crawled over to her. He threw her legs up over his shoulders, hands grabbing her ass cheeks. He rubbed his face over her inner thigh, making her squeal a little, laughing. He brought his hands up and spread her lips, exposing her clit to the air. She shivered a little and he licked a path from the bottom of her lips all the way up to her clit, circling it once with his tongue before rubbing his scruffy chin over her clit.

"Oh god, Rolf. Do that again. Yes, yes, there. Oh shit!" Shaye yelled as Rolf surged up and impaled her on his dick. He held her wrists above her head, alternating between nipping at her nipples and kissing her like the world was about to end. *'Bite me again, please...love...I need it...love you...make me come,'* she babbled at him. His thrusts were speeding up, nice and hard the way she liked it. She was right on the edge when she felt his teeth in her neck again. She came so hard that she thought she saw stars. She felt the flood of warmth in her depths and heard his groan of completion. He lay down next to her and they fell asleep in each other's arms.

A knock on their door woke them up. "I totally don't want to interrupt, but it's almost lunchtime. I was thinking of going into town and checking it out."

Shaye laughed. "Let us get a quick shower and we'll go with you and show you around. I'm starving. We can grab lunch in town. Give us about twenty minutes," she shouted through the door.

"We can stop at Sam's for lunch and introduce Tess to the guys," Rolfston added as he headed to the bathroom.

Shaye and Rolf grabbed a quick shower and got dressed. There were lots of little touches here and there, a few quick kisses. It was weird, but Shaye could feel Rolf even more now that they had completed the mate bond. She didn't have to focus as much to talk to him either.

"Sam's brewery has great burgers and I am addicted to his fries. They're perfectly crunchy on the outside and soft on the inside. Yum," Shaye told Tess as they walked to the car.

"Well, it sounds like a great place to grab lunch then," Tess agreed. She felt antsy and drawn down to the town today.

"Are you okay?" Shaye asked as they parked the car. "You seem fidgety today."

"Yeah, just antsy. I had a dream last night, maybe a mate? He had green eyes. And a dog, I think? I may pick up some ear plugs while we're in town too," she teased Shaye, wiggling her eyebrows.

"Stop it! We weren't that loud. Plus, I know the walls are insulated really well," she scolded laughingly. To Rolf she thought, *'Well, now we definitely have to go to Sam's for lunch.'*

'Yup. He's not going to know what hit him.' Rolf grinned.

They walked through town and showed Tess their favorite spots. She loved the bookstore and could see hanging out there or even getting some work done at the café. She really enjoyed being able to work remotely in different areas. It would be good for when she needed a break from the house. She was charmed by Berkley and they got along well. He had some amazing pieces for sale.

Tess was already planning on coming back and getting some items to ship back home for Christmas gifts.

"Hey, Berkley, we were heading down to Sam's next, if you want to join us for lunch," she heard Rolf offer.

"Sure," Berkley agreed.

They waited while he closed up his shop and put the "Out To Lunch" sign up in the door.

Walking down the street, Tess paused as she saw the sign for the brewery. "Wait a minute. Berkley, you're a Fae and you named your place the Winged Potter. Sam's place is called Black Wolf Brewery? Is he a shifter? Could you be any more obvious?" she asked with a laugh.

Rolf laughed with her. "That's what I told them when they opened. But they both insisted no one would pay attention. Those who would were probably paranormals or knew about us already. And they were right, no one really paid attention to the names."

Shaye opened the door and went in first. She wanted to see Sam's face when he smelled Tess for the first time. And that was a sentence she never thought she would say, she thought to herself.

"Hey, Shaye! Usual table?" Sam asked as he spotted her from the hallway to his office.

"We have four today, five if you want to join us."

"I think I can sit with you guys for a bit," Sam said as he walked closer.

Shaye, Rolf, and Berkley watched in amusement, and happiness for their friends, as Sam finally smelled Tess's scent. His nostrils flared and he looked around looking for the source. Shaye moved out of the way so he could see Tess. Tess took one look at Sam and squealed. She ran to him, jumping into his arms. Luckily Sam caught her.

"Hi," Tess said.

"Hi," Sam replied, staring at her.

"Oh boy. Sam, this is my friend Tess. Tess, this is our friend Sam."

"Nice to meet you, Mate. Would you like to come to my place to talk?" Sam asked. At her nod, he shouted to his staff that he was leaving and was not to be disturbed.

"I'll see you later, Shaye! Don't wait up." Tess waved madly as Sam carried her to the back where the stairs to his apartment were located.

The people who were in the restaurant burst into laughter. Most of them there at the moment were paranormals and knew what had just happened.

"Well, I guess we should just seat ourselves," Rolf said as he laughed. "I'll go check in with the kitchen and see if they need me to call anyone to help."

Shaye and Berkley sat by the corner gas fireplace, enjoying the atmosphere. It didn't put off much heat, but it was nice to look at. Rolf came to sit with them. "I put in our usual orders before the lunch crowd comes in. They are going to call in another server to help while Sam is...indisposed."

"I'm so happy for them," Berkley said. "Thanks for asking me to come. It's not often you get to see your friends find their mates."

"It's going to happen for you too, Berkley. I know it," Shaye reassured him.

The next month passed in a blur. They got into a loose routine. They would eat breakfast together before Shaye would go to work. Rolfston would walk or drive her to work and pick her up. They would hang out with friends, especially on the weekends. Sam and Berkley were hanging around the house more, and they could usually be found outside in the hammocks. Tess and Sam split their time between the house and his apartment attached to the brewery. They were a great couple together, although it was funny to listen to her complain about dog hair on the furniture.

It was easy to get complacent when things were going so well.

7

Shaye came home uneasy. The hospital was starting to really get to her. The pain there seemed overwhelming most days, and she couldn't figure out why. A new orderly had recently started, and he was extremely unpleasant to be near. Ever since he started, her feelings had been almost amplified. She caught him watching her several times this week. One time it looked like he was taking her picture. There was nothing concrete that she could complain to her supervisor about though. Her instincts were telling her he was bad news, but there wasn't much she could do about it.

"You were quiet the whole way home. Is everything alright?" Rolf asked, handing her what smelled like chamomile tea in her mug.

"Kind of. We had a new employee start last week, an orderly. There is nothing I can prove, but I've been uneasy since he came. I find him staring at me, almost like he's following me sometimes. I try to never be alone with him, but he was just assigned to my floor today. It's really weird; since he started, the hospital has been overwhelming. It's like it has multiplied somehow. We have the same patients, a few new ones, but nothing so extreme that I would have this much trouble shielding myself at work. After we completed our mating, it seemed like my shields got a little stronger, so I'm not sure why it is so hard to control it now," she tried to explain. It was all a feeling; it was hard to explain without having any proof.

"I trust your instincts, never doubt that," he reassured her. "Have I seen him before?"

"No, he's always gone by the time you come to pick me up."

"Let's have Berkley stop by tomorrow and see if he can't get a read on him. He can't always tell if a person is gifted or a paranormal, but he is really good at telling if they have good intentions or not. Let me give him a call." Rolf kissed the top of her head and grabbed his phone.

Shaye was doing her rounds, checking on her patients, when she felt eyes on her again. Looking around, she saw Dan, the orderly, staring right at her. He wasn't even pretending not to look. There was no one else around and it was really creeping her out.

The elevator dinged and she gave a sigh of relief. She almost tackled Berkley when she saw him step out.

"Hey, Shaye. I was visiting a friend and thought I would see if you wanted to grab coffee with us," Berkley offered.

"I have five more minutes until my lunch break, and then I would love to," she responded.

"Great. I'll wait for you here then."

She knew then that Berkley had read something bad on the other man, the one who scurried away quickly. Her watch buzzed, signaling it was her break time, and she walked back over to Berkley. "I can go now."

"Let's go to my shop. I have something I want to give you."

She grabbed her purse and followed him to the Winged Potter. He locked the front door after them and led her into the back room.

"He's definitely bad news," Berkley said as he searched around in his drawers. "I can't get a good read on him, but I'm leaning toward vampire. He is not there to help anyone. I do think he is somehow amplifying the pain that is at the hospital. I think it is to target you, but I can't be sure. Ah ha! Found it," he shouted as he pulled out a pendant. "I made this so long ago, that I forgot about it, or I would have given it to you when I gave you the mugs. This is spelled for magical protection; it should stop you from feeling the amplifications and repel any magical attacks. It will only keep harmful magic from you, not the magic that is trying to help you like the mugs or Rolf's biting pheromones." He winked at her.

"Thank you, Berkley. You are a great friend."

Berkley looked like he was thinking something over. "I know you love to help people, and I don't want you to have to stop. I can't ward the hospital though, so I can't do too much more than the pendant. Public places of healing like that are off limits. I know Dr. T has been talking about hiring a nurse. Since it is his private practice and he is a paranormal, I could get his permission to ward his building, if you would be interested in changing jobs. Please tell me if I'm overstepping and to shut up."

Shaye thought about it. Even with Berkley's protection pendant, she wasn't sure she would be comfortable at the hospital if Dan was still there. Her gut told her to avoid him.

'*Love, what's wrong?*' She heard Rolf ask anxiously.

'*I'm fine. I'm at Berkley's. The orderly was staring at me again today. Berkley brought me back to his shop to give me a pendant. He mentioned that Dr. T may be hiring. I think he's encouraging me, not so subtly, to change jobs.'*

'I can see his reasoning. He's usually right, but never tell him I said that. I will support whatever you want to do, love.'

'I'll stop in and see Dr. T before I head back to the hospital. You're still going to pick me up?'

'Yes. I'll make sure to get there a few minutes early.'

'Thank you. Love you,' she replied.

'Always, love.'

Berkley was grinning at her. "How is Rolf?"

Shaye laughed. "Good. Sorry, I haven't perfected my "I look like I'm paying attention, but I'm totally just talking to my Mate" face."

"It's fine. I hope to one day have the same problem," Berkley said a little sadly.

She gave him a hug. "Rolf didn't want me to tell you, but he thinks you are right and I should talk to Dr. T," she told him to cheer him up, happy when he laughed.

"I'll walk you down and wait. Once you're done, I'll walk you back to the hospital. I think Dr. T is going to give you a job right away; you would be a great help and his practice has certainly picked up as more people have moved here."

He was right. Again. Shaye talked to the older man for a few minutes about what his expectations were. She made sure to tell him about why she was thinking about leaving the hospital, and he assured her that Berkley could ward the office. As she shook his hand, accepting the job, he got a faraway look on his face.

"The other benefit about working here, is the flexible hours. If you need to, you can always go part-time in the future," he told her.

"Thank you," she responded, a little confused.

Berkley just laughed at her when she told him. "He sometimes gets visions, I think, but it's no use trying to get the information out of him. I've tried for years. Someday you will just look back, and be like 'Oh, that's what he meant!' I'm glad you got the job; it will be a much better fit. Do you need me to stay at the hospital with you until Rolf comes?"

"No, I think I should be fine. There will be more staff around this afternoon. Plus, I have your pendant now. I'll go give my notice to my supervisor when I get in. I hate to do it on short notice, but I really don't want to stay there. I can't explain it either, since she's human and doesn't know about the paranormals here in town."

Her boss was understandably upset that she was leaving, but at least a new nurse was supposed to start in a couple of days, so they wouldn't be short-staffed. Shaye just felt relief that she would be at a place where she could be more herself and not hide her gifts quite as much. Dr. T seemed like he would be a good boss. She felt lighter as she walked out to meet Rolf at the front doors.

"How did it go?" he asked.

"Pretty good. Dr. T offered me the job and I gave my notice here. Berkley is going to set wards around Dr. T's building. I'm actually excited. I think this will be a good fit. It will be a smaller amount of people, but I can still use my gift. Maybe even more, since some patients are paranormal and are used to people having gifts or magic."

"We should celebrate! What do you want to do?"

'Hmm…how about a bath and you can eat…me…' she suggested.

Shaye screamed in laughter as he picked her up and used his vampire speed to run home. Barely pausing to lock the front door, he ran her up the stairs and had a bath going.

'That is a handy skill to have,' she teased him as she started to unbutton his shirt.

He drew her face to his and kissed her. She could feel his love and hunger. His fangs were already peeking out and she shivered. *'Clothes off now,'* she pleaded and then gasped as he simply ripped her shirt in half. Laughing, she told him, "Not my pants! I like these ones."

"Hurry up, then. I'm already done," he bragged.

"Not all of us have vampire speed," she said pertly. She reached out, tracing a finger down his body until she reached his cock. It was already hard for her, a drop of precum at the tip. Glancing up at him, she dropped to her knees and teasingly licked a stripe from the base to the tip. He groaned watching her. Shaye made sure to look into his eyes as she teasingly ran her tongue up the center again and around each side. As she finally took him in her mouth, she sucked him in and continued to lick back and forth with her tongue. It was his favorite sensation; her mouth tight and wet around his dick, her tongue sweeping broad caresses against him. His hands were holding her hair so he could watch her, but she could also feel his hands caressing her breasts. Her nipples were hard, begging for attention. His invisible fingers pinched them, then traveled down her stomach to her opening. She was already wet for him, her lips puffy and open, ready for him to fill her. Her cunt clenched, wanting his hot hard length inside her. *'Now. Please. I need you,'* she told him.

'In a minute, love. I believe you mentioned something about eating and I haven't had a taste yet.'

He pulled her up, kissing her deeply. A finger slipped between her lips, stroking her clit. It was amazing, but still not enough. He picked her up and sat her on the counter. Leaning back, she spread her legs and watched as he bent down to lick her. A few fingers thrust into her and she was overwhelmed with the stimulation. He knew exactly how to get her close. She felt a fang gently graze over her clit and she orgasmed. Rolf lapped up the wetness leaking from her cunt and brought her closer to the end of the counter. Wrapping her legs around his waist, she pulled him in, his dick finally filling her. He kept one hand playing with her clit, while he wrapped the other one behind her head and pulled her in for a kiss.

'Gentle or hard?' he asked.

'I need hard today,' she replied.

He started thrusting into her, his shaft throbbing inside of her, deep and hard. He grabbed her hips and tilted her up, hitting her G-spot perfectly. He used his powers to stroke her clit, flicking it a little at the end. When she felt his balls pull up against his body, she pulled him in tighter and turned her head, showing him her neck. *'Bite me, love. Drink and make me come again.'* As his teeth broke through her skin, she felt another orgasm rush through her. She vaguely felt him drinking as she floated on the rush of endorphins.

Coming back to herself, she realized they were cuddled up in the bathtub. The water was still warm and there were now candles lit on the counter.

"I love bath time," Rolf said smugly. Well, he did make her orgasm twice, so he probably had a little right to be smug, she thought to herself.

"Me too." Shaye rested against his chest, allowing the warm water to relax her and let the day sink away. As they soaked, they held hands and talked about the coming weekend and their plans. Some days she couldn't believe how lucky she was. She had a mate, friends, a home, and now a job she thought she would really love. Not bad for someone whose parents had kicked her out of the house for being different.

8

S haye was exhausted. She loved working for Dr. T, but this week ended in the full moon and all the paranormals seemed to have lost their minds. Rolf wasn't kidding when he said the werewolves got hyper, but what he failed to mention was that they also did crazy things like try skateboarding for the first time and breaking an arm or picking fights with each other. Although, it seemed like there were more outsiders in the clinic this week. Rolf had been extremely horny this week too, not that she was complaining, but she was running on less sleep than normal. Tess kept popping in, checking on her. She couldn't tell Shaye what it was, just a feeling that something was going to happen. Shaye was going to be so happy when the weekend came tomorrow.

'Love, can you ask Dr. T if I can get some bags for this weekend? After our mating, I asked him to wait, but I think it's time I had some on hand,' Rolf asked her.

'Why? I can feed you,' Shaye responded, a little hurt that he didn't want to drink from her.

'You're exhausted by this week. Berkley's mugs have helped a lot, but you are still run-down and I don't want to make it

*even worse. Let's sleep in this weekend to recharge, and I'll
enjoy you on Monday, okay? I'm a little hungrier during the
full moon, just not as bad as the werewolves,'* he said as he
laughed.

'Alright, I'll ask him for some,' she replied. *'But I better
feel your teeth come Monday!'* Shaye demanded. She smiled
as she felt an invisible kiss on his favorite spot to bite on
her neck. She had become addicted to feeling his teeth in
her neck during sex; it enhanced all the sensations her
nerve endings were already feeling and always resulted
in an orgasm. Most of the time, he only took a sip or two,
not needing to have a full feeding with how much they
were intimate with each other.

Walking over to Dr. T's office, she knocked on the
door frame and peeked her head in.

"Morning, Dr. T. Rolf wanted to know if you had any
bags on hand that he could get for this weekend?"

"Hmmm. I don't think I do. I'll place a rush order
over at the hospital for him. It should be here by the end
of your shift, so you won't have to come back. Is everything alright?" he questioned, concerned.

"Yup, everyone is healthy. He just thought I was too
tired to drink from this weekend and wanted the bagged
blood to have on hand. He said he gets a little hungrier
during the full moon, but not as hungry as the werewolves," she joked.

"Ah, well, I don't think many people outeat the
wolves. Everyone gets a little hungrier during the full
moon."

"Why is that?"

"We're not entirely sure. I know you've heard the
expression 'it's the full moon' to explain weird things,
but it does seem to hold some truth. Humans can be
affected, but the paranormals definitely feel it. It seems
to increase the prey drive in the predators. Most of them

will just go about their daily lives, but eat a little more to satisfy the hunger, run with their Packs or Clans to get rid of their extra energy. The witches will often use the time to make a few potions, tend to their herb gardens, and have a feast with their family group. Each paranormal has a little bit of a different way of celebrating, but it usually involves eating more and lots of activity. It's the teenagers who normally cause most of the problems; they are filled with hormones as it is and then the full moon amplifies it. We'll see more arguments and fights break out, but the great thing about this town being full of knowing humans and mixes of paranormals, is that we can all help keep them in check until they learn to control it by themselves. It never gets bad, but we are seeing a lot more out-of-towners this week, and they seem to be the majority of patients coming in. Speaking of..." He trailed off as they heard the bell over the clinic door ding. The receptionist called back and let them know it was for a set of stiches. "Can you handle this one and I'll call the hospital to get some bags sent over?"

The rest of the day flowed pretty easily, although there was a rush right before closing. People must be trying to get in before the weekend when the clinic was closed, she thought. The end of the day finally came and she was anticipating soaking in the bathtub. Maybe a glass of wine and some chocolate to go with it. She could pick up dinner on the way home, something easy.

"Shaye, the hospital dropped off the blood. It's in the fridge in a cooler bag," Dr. T reminded her.

"I didn't even know they dropped it off," she replied, surprised. Normally they had the doctor or her sign off on the delivery.

"Sherri said it was during that last rush. They let her sign for it since we were so busy."

"Thank you. I'll see you on Monday then, have a great weekend!" Shaye replied as she headed to the fridge.

Rolf was waiting for her outside. "Hey, beautiful," he said, giving her a soft kiss. "You ready to head home?"

"I was thinking we should pick something up for dinner, something easy to make or reheat."

"I threw some stuff in the slow cooker this afternoon. I'm hoping it turns out to be a nice stew, but if it's horrible, we can always order a pizza in."

"Sounds great. I was thinking we could have a soak in the tub? I am ready for some TV binge-watching and relaxing this weekend."

They headed back to the house, the air quiet. It was a nice night, still a little warm in the evenings. "Maybe we can sit out back and have a fire tonight, snuggle on the couch," Shaye suggested.

"That sounds nice. After your bath though," Rolf added. "Then you'll be ready to just relax. I know Sam is at the brewery for a little bit, but he mentioned going out for a run, so he might pop in. Tess said she was going to help serve, they had someone call in sick tonight. We'll have the house to ourselves for a while." He winked at her.

The slow cooker was filling the house with a nice beef stew smell. Shaye couldn't wait to try it for dinner. She thought they still had a loaf of bread from the bakery left too. Winner, winner, yummy dinner, she giggled to herself.

"The bath is ready, head on up and get started. I'm going to have a quick snack before I join you. I don't want to be tempted to bite you," Rolf added as he gave her a kiss on her neck.

She shivered. That spot was definitely a hot spot now. "Hurry then. Love you, thank you for the bath," she added as she rushed up the stairs. She heard the microwave ding as she entered the bathroom. The water was steamy, and it looked like he had placed a glass of wine for her on the edge, along with a few candles. Best mate ever!

Shaye was about to climb into the tub when she heard a crash downstairs, followed by a searing pain in her stomach. Throwing on a robe, she ran down the stairs. *'Rolf, Rolf, what's wrong?'* she cried out in panic. She could feel the pain from her mate. She skidded into the kitchen finding Rolf on the floor, pale white, sweating, a broken cup on the floor with blood splattered around it.

'No, love! Don't touch it!' Rolf shouted. *'Something's wrong with it. Call Dr. T and everyone. I love you...'* He trailed off, his voice weakening with each word.

She grabbed his hand, focusing on his body. Something was tearing him apart from the inside. Shaye leaned up, never letting go of Rolf, and grabbed her phone off the table.

Her hands shaking, she used the voice automated calling. "Call Tess," she told the phone, putting most of her focus on trying to slow down the progression of what was trying to kill Rolf.

"Hey, lady! Are you guys having fun? What are you doing for the full—" Tess started.

"Tess! Rolf's dying. I need help. Grab Dr. T and the guys. I need you here now. I don't know what to do," she sobbed.

"We're coming. We're not going to let him go," Tess promised.

After what felt like hours, but was probably only a couple of minutes, she heard the sound of running paws and saw Sam's large black wolf slide through the doggie door that Rolf had just installed. He had done it to tease Sam, but it was useful when Sam was in wolf form. He came over to Shaye and Rolf, sniffing all along Rolf. He gave Shaye a quick nuzzle before trotting over to sniff the fallen mug and remaining blood. He sneezed at the scent, pulling his lips back from his teeth in a snarl.

"Shaye! We're here. Dr. T is coming right behind us. He was stopping to get some supplies from the clinic. Oh shit," Tess whispered as she came into kitchen, Berkley right behind her.

Berkley started running his hands over Rolf's fallen body, his eyes closed in concentration.

"What happened?" Tess asked, putting an arm around her friend. She also was trying to scan Rolf to see what was causing the damage.

"I got off work and we came back to the house. He made me a bath," Shaye recounted, tears falling from her eyes. "He stayed downstairs to get a snack, a drink. I heard a crash and felt this immense pain in my stomach. I found him like this."

Shaye kept hold of her mate, willing her strength into him. All of her healing and it didn't seem to make too much of a difference. She didn't even look up as Doc came into the room.

"Crap," she heard the doctor mutter. "What the hell happened?"

Tess answered for Shaye. "Came home, Shaye went upstairs, Rolf stayed downstairs to drink. He must have fallen; Shaye heard a crash, felt stomach pain, found him here."

Berkley looked up. "It's not magical from what I can tell."

Tess nodded. "I'm not sensing anything either."

Sam whined. He was still standing by the debris. "Sam, get back please. Rolf told me not to touch it," Shaye warned. "No!" she shouted as she saw him lick a splatter.

Suddenly, there was a naked Sam in her kitchen, running his tongue under the faucet.

"He said it's poisoned," Tess said. "That was extremely stupid of you!" she yelled at her mate.

Berkley left the room, coming back with a pair of Rolf's sweatpants for Sam. "Thanks," Sam said. After putting them on, he turned to face the group. "It's definitely been poisoned. There is an acidity to it that shouldn't be there. My tongue is not happy."

"Come here," Shaye said. She touched Sam. She could feel very faint traces of what was poisoning Rolf. She placed a little bit of her focus on Sam for a minute, able to help rid his body of most of it. "That should help enough for your natural healing to finish the rest." She pulled all her gift back into Rolf. His breathing was getting labored, his heartbeat a little erratic.

Dr. T had been drawing samples of Rolf's blood. Bending over, he used his penlight to examine his eyes. The pupils were dilated. When he opened Rolf's mouth, his tongue was redder than normal, and not just from the blood he had consumed. Doc stood up and placed the vials in a cooler, along with the other bags of blood that they had brought home from work. "Let's try and get him in a bed for now. I don't know that the hospital is the best place right now, since that's where the blood came from. I can set up most of what we might need right now and run into the clinic to get anything else we might need. As soon as we get him set up with a saline IV, I'll take these samples to someone I trust. The results should be back quickly."

"Berkley and I can carry him up. Tess, can you run up and get the bed ready? Put him in their bed, Shaye's scent will help keep him focused on his mate. It'll give him something to fight for. Shaye, can you stay with us on the stairs? I know you don't want to let him go." Sam directed everyone.

It was a slow procession up the stairs. Tess and Doc had run ahead to get the room ready. Sam and Berkley carried Rolf up the stairs slowly. Sam was carrying Rolf under the arms, while Berkley had him under his knees. Shaye was holding a foot. They must have looked ridiculous, she thought a little hysterically. When they got into the room, Tess had the bed turned down, but there were absorbent pads lining one side of the bed. Doc had an IV stand set up next to the bed and was running a saline line.

"Lay him here," Dr. T indicated. "Can you help hold him up so that I can get his shirt off? Shaye, you keep sending him healing. Pace yourself. This is probably going to be a long process. Let me get the saline line in," he said as he moved around Sam. "I don't want to guess at which antidotes to use, but the saline may help," he explained as he worked. "Tess, grab the black bottle from my bag. It should say Activated Charcoal Solution on it. Thanks," he said, taking it from her. "It's been less than an hour, Shaye?" he questioned.

She nodded. "I think so?"

Tess looked up from her phone. "It's been twenty-five minutes since she called."

"Great, then we can try to get this solution in him. The charcoal should help keep his body from absorbing more of the poison. We can give him a few doses if we need to. Berkley, hold his head back for me. Sam, make sure he stays upright. Let's see if we can't get him to swallow on his own without having to use a tube. Shaye, talk to him and try to get him to swallow."

Shaye nodded. *'Mate, Dr. T is here. He's going to give you something to drink, try to swallow it down. Otherwise, he has to tube you and get the solution to your stomach that way.'*

She felt a faint stirring through their connection, but no other response.

"He's not really responding, but I did tell him to swallow it."

Doc nodded and slowly managed to get a dose down Rolf's throat and had them lay him down onto the bed.

"We'll give him another dose in a half hour. For a human, it would be two hours, but I'm betting on vampire increased healing to need it a lot sooner. I'll call my contact at the hospital and have them check the security footage to see if we can get anything that would help us," Doc added as he started out the door. "I'll be back as soon as I drop off the blood for testing. Shaye, if I'm not back in time, get another dose down him. If he can't swallow, intubate and administer that way."

The group of friends sat around his bedside. There didn't seem to be any change, but he wasn't worse either. Shaye kept pushing her healing into her mate, hoping that it would help.

"Shaye, have you eaten yet?"

Shaye shook her head.

"Sam, can you run down to the kitchen and bring back bowls of the stew for everyone?" Tess asked.

As Sam went to leave the room, Berkley added, "Bring Shaye a water too, but use the blue mug I gave her. It should help."

"I'm not very hungry," Shaye said. She was too worried to feel any hunger. She just wanted to focus on her mate.

"I know," Tess answered. "You still have to eat a bowl. It will help keep your energy levels up. I don't know how long you can keep using your gift. You normally don't use it non-stop for long periods of time. I grabbed a power bag I had made earlier today," she said, pulling a satchel out of her pocket. "Hold this in one hand, it should help with your gift."

"What's in it?" Shaye asked curiously.

"A diamond for love, power, and to amplify. Amber for focus. Opal to help if we need to do spell work and as your birthstone it should help bolster you as well. Amethyst for healing, focus, and to help center your energy. Moonstone to help with healing, and to promote our bonds of friendship. Topaz to avoid danger. Turquoise for Rolf's birthstone, healing, and for protection from negativity. And you can't go wrong with quartz. Probably a bit of an overkill, but it will cover all our bases. This would be helpful to carry for everyday use too. I made it small enough to fit in a pocket. Or maybe we can get it made into a pendant. If you do carry it full-time though, you should know that moonstone also helps promote fertility, so you may want to take that one out," Tess added.

Sam came back into the room carrying a bunch of bowls on a serving tray. Berkley moved a nightstand over to act as a side table so Shaye could eat easier.

Berkley laid a hand on Rolf's head. "His pain is so strong."

Shaye was startled. She had thought her mate had gone numb, she couldn't feel anything. Maybe it was the crystals protecting her? No, she thought, she hadn't been overwhelmed since she entered the kitchen. She had been so focused on trying to heal him, that she didn't notice the lack of pain. Looking closely at their mate bond, she could see where he had blocked part of it. "That asshole," she blurted out.

"Who?" Berkley asked, confused.

"Rolf. He's using up energy blocking the pain from me."

"One of his powers is shielding, so I don't think it's

taking too much from him right now," Sam tried to reassure her.

Shaye managed to get a couple mugs full of water and a bowl of soup down. She did feel a little better now that she had eaten. Tess had gone downstairs to make a pot of coffee for everyone. They all felt that Rolfston was holding steady. They had about five minutes left until his next dosage when suddenly it all went to hell.

9

S uddenly, Rolf started convulsing. Sam and Berkley rushed over to make sure he didn't fall off the bed. Shaye grabbed his wrist to monitor his heart rate. It was erratic and he was struggling to breath.

Doc rushed in. "Situation?"

"Five minutes remaining until next dose. He just started to seize, heart rate and breathing erratic and labored," Shaye answered while watching to make sure he didn't tear out his IV.

Doc took over monitoring his heart rate. As the seizure slowed down, Doc barked out, "He's going to crash. Get ready for chest compressions. Sam, you help me. I'll compress, you breathe. Shaye, you push as hard as you can, all your healing right now."

Shaye's own heart about stopped beating when she saw Rolf wasn't breathing anymore. Grabbing the crystal bag, she made herself breathe and focus on her mate bond. She grabbed hold of it in her mind. *'Not today, Mate. You stay with me. We have things to do still. You promised me a bite on Monday. Don't make me lose you. I want forever with you. I can't have that if you're gone and can't turn me. I'd be so alone.'* Shaye bribed, promised, and cajoled with every fiber of her being, pushing every bit of healing power she could muster. She felt Tess and Berkley step up behind her and put their hands on her shoulders. She could feel them pushing their own powers toward her. She felt Doc pushing his own type of healing power at her mate. She didn't realize he had a healing gift, she thought as she started to get lightheaded. She kept pushing. With all the other powers rushing through her, she wouldn't die from pushing too hard, she reasoned. She held on until Doc breathed a sigh of relief. "We've got him back," she heard him say as she blacked out.

Waking up, Shaye realized she was lying on the bed next to Rolf. He was breathing easier, his heartbeat regular. Sitting up, she noticed that Sam was sleeping in wolf form at the end of the bed by Rolf's feet. Berkley was asleep in the chair, Tess asleep in a pile of blankets on the floor.

Shaye leaned over to give Rolf a kiss. *'Stay with me, Mate. I'll be right back, I just have to run to the bathroom.'*

Shaye saw herself in the mirror and realized that she had been in her robe this entire time. She brushed her teeth and got dressed. Coming out of the room, she saw Doc coming back in. He had a tray full of breakfast items and coffee.

"How are you feeling today, Shaye?" Doc asked.

She couldn't believe that she passed out wearing only her robe in front of her boss. "I'm good. I actually feel so much better than I normally do after an intense healing, although I don't think I've ever done one quite like

Rolf's. How is he today? His breathing and heart rate seem normal."

"He's still unconscious, but no additional seizures. His pupils are still a little dilated and there is a little redness remaining to his mouth. He seems stable though. I've changed out the saline and gave another dose of the activated charcoal once I knew he was done with the seizure. You seem in pretty good health today too. I think you pushed really hard yesterday and the influx of additional power overloaded you. I would recommend you take it easy, but I have a feeling you would just ignore me. Not that I blame you; if it were my mate that was ill, I would probably do the same thing. Unless we can find out what caused this, I'm afraid that we just keep doing what we have been. I have a friend bringing fresh blood bags in. They're going to test them before bringing them over just to be safe. I'll check them out again once they are here and Sam can give them a sniff. Rolfston needs to drink, but while you're still focused on healing him, it shouldn't be from you."

Shaye nodded. She grabbed a cup of coffee and a bowl of granola. "Thank you for breakfast."

She watched as Sam's nose started to twitch in his sleep. He must have smelled the bacon on the tray, she laughingly thought to herself. Once he was fully awake, he jumped off the bed to stretch. He checked on Rolf, head-nudged Shaye and headed out the door. "Huh," Shaye said, surprised. "I thought he would have gone for the bacon."

"He will," Tess answered, sitting up. "He ran to get changed. I'm going to grab a shower, unless you need me?"

"I think we're good right now. Thank you for watching over him," Shaye told her.

"We're family," Tess answered simply as she gave Shaye a hug and followed after her mate.

Berkley was the last one sleeping, but he looked exhausted. "Is Berkley alright? He looks worn out."

"He and Tess both added their own magic to the healing, and I think he pushed himself pretty hard as well. Healing is not his strong suit," Doc replied.

Shaye got up, grabbed one of the blankets from Tess's pile and covered Berkley up. She gave him a quick check and pushed a little healing energy his way. She didn't want her friends to suffer because they had helped Rolf.

Dr. T's phone started ringing. "Sorry, I'll take this out in the hallway so I don't wake him."

Tess and Sam returned a few minutes later and sat down to eat their breakfast. Between the three of them, they drained the coffee carafe. "I'll go make another pot," Tess offered. "I feel like I should ask Doc if I can just get a coffee IV." Shaye totally agreed with that statement.

"Nope, sorry. A coffee IV is bad for you. You'll just have to get your caffeination the traditional way," Doc said as he came back in the room, waking Berkley up. "Sorry to wake you, but I thought you'd want to hear the news. That was my contact from the hospital. It appears that Dan, the orderly, sent the blood supply over from the hospital. The hospital's security camera caught him injecting something into the bags that Rolf ordered. We can tell he contaminated them, but we're still waiting on the tests to come back to see what with. He used someone else to deliver them, since I had made it clear he wasn't welcome at the clinic. Sherri didn't recognize the delivery man, although he did have a hospital ID badge," Dr. T told Shaye. "We gave the footage from both the hospital and the clinic to the Sheriff. There's a warrant out for both of them."

Tess was confused. "Rolf is a vampire. How are you going to explain all of this to the Sheriff? If he was human, I don't think he would have survived. Plus, we didn't bring him to the hospital or call 911, so it's going to look suspicious."

"The Sheriff is a shifter," Sam chimed in. "Not sure what kind, but he's dealt with trouble paranormals before. He acts as a human Sheriff and a paranormal Warden."

Doc nodded. "Right now, the public human-friendly warrant is for tampering with hospital supplies, selling and distributing known contaminated blood with the intent to harm. The paranormal warrant will have the totality of the crimes listed for other Wardens to see."

"What's a Warden?" Shaye asked.

"Basically a paranormal police officer. They have Wardens throughout the country. Criminals are brought to the holding cells underneath the real jails. They have reinforced bars, magical wards, things to keep the ones under arrest inside. Someone with the gift of TruthSpeak will come and cast judgement."

"Shouldn't there be a jury?"

"These people can tell if someone is telling the truth, when they are lying, what they are hiding. It's a power not many have, one that many fear. They can look into your mind and see everything you are. It's assumed that they will know the truth and cast the right judgement," Berkley added.

"And none of these Truth people have been wrong before? Or lied for some reason?" Shaye asked incredulously.

"It's considered an honor to hold this position. There was one incident a few hundred years ago of someone abusing their power. There is now a witch from a local group that will meet the TruthSpeaker and make sure everything is done honestly. I believe they cast a truth spell over the group and have a spelled crystal that will glow when the person holding it is lying. Each member involved in the judgement holds one of these crystals," Doc answered. "Anyway, once they find Dan and his accomplice, the Sheriff has the ability to arrest them, the jail to hold them, and then someone who can punish them.

"The good news is that people are looking for them. We also should have the blood tests soon. The bad news is that his symptoms point to a few different poisons, most of which do not have an antidote. If that is the case, we will just have to keep treating the symptoms."

"Why didn't the wards pick up on the poisoned blood?" Shaye asked, confused.

"The wards were meant to keep out a person, shifter, human, etcetera. The blood wasn't spelled, so the wards didn't pick up on any evil magic. We were so focused on keeping out an evil being and magic that we didn't even stop to think about an inanimate object. The blood itself isn't cognizant, right? Most poisons exist in nature; they're not harmful just by being there, they have to be ingested or touched for them to have an effect. And even then, the plant isn't choosing to be mean, it is simply its nature and isn't actively trying to harm, it just wants to exist. Take poison ivy for example: you can look at it and even walk by it without being affected. Some people can touch it and not have any reaction. The plant isn't trying to hurt anyone, it's just there. I'm sure it exists in the woods on the grounds.

"Tess and I are working on a way to enhance the wards so that things brought with the intent to harm won't be able to come in, but that can get tricky too. If we leave it as a broad 'anything that harms cannot come in' type of thing, then even simple things like pepper spray wouldn't be able to pass the wards, much less some of Tess's potions or spells. It would be protecting us, the intent behind the things would be to cause harm, so the wards would keep it out even though we want it in. I think we can create it to where we can have the wards keep out things meant to harm **us**, but we have to get the wording just right in order to get the result we want," Berkley tried to explain.

"We're working on it," Tess reassured her. "I sent a request out to my family to see if they knew of any spells that would work for this type of scenario. All of us have witch and Fae friends scattered throughout the world, so we're hoping some of them might have learned something that could help too."

A few hours later, Doc's phone rang again. He stayed in the room this time since everyone was awake, besides Rolf who hadn't stirred at all. He greeted the caller and then listened for several minutes. "Are you sure? Did you rerun the tests? Okay, thank you."

He looked at them. "He was poisoned. Unfortunately, it was quite the cocktail and none of the poisons have an antidote. We will keep treating the symptoms and keep his fluids up. Once the blood arrives, we'll get him to drink. I want him to drink at least a few times a day, hopefully using the mug Berkley made to help bolster his energy. Any amount will help dilute and flush out the toxins. His vampire healing will need fresh blood to stay strong enough to fight the poison."

"Which poisons?" Shaye asked quietly.

Doc winced. "White snakeroot, nightshade, wolfsbane, and ricin. The ricin isn't as easy to obtain either, so the Sheriff is trying to find some leads that way. Unfortunately, anyone can buy the other plants or even find them out in nature. They're not native everywhere, but someone could have collected them."

Shaye grabbed Sam's hand, searching his body for any lingering side effects. She knew wolfsbane was especially poisonous for the werewolves. She gave Tess a smile when she didn't find anything. "All clear."

It was a week before Rolf woke up. A week of worrying and sleeping beside him, holding on to his hand to make sure he didn't get worse. Tess, Sam, and Berkley moved into the house, but went back to work after a few days of no change. Tess did work mainly from the house though. Doc came over every day after the clinic closed to check on him. He gave her the time off to watch over Rolf and limited the clinic to local paranormals only so that he could handle the workload with just him and Sherri, the receptionist.

Shaye was sitting in the recliner Sam had moved into the room for her. The other chair wasn't comfortable for long-term sitting. She tried to stay in the room as much as she could, but she did go downstairs for meals. Sometimes everyone would eat in their bedroom, trying to include Rolf in the conversation to bring him back.

"Ow. Fuck. What's wrong with my dick?" she heard him rasp as he tried to get out of bed.

"Stop! Lie back down. You have a catheter in. You've been unconscious for a week now," Shaye told him as she raced to his side of the bed to help him lie down. '*I am so glad to see your eyes, Mate. You scared me so much. I love you.*'

'*I love you too. What happened? I remember you getting ready for your bath. I had guzzled some blood because I was in a hurry to join you. I didn't finish the cup, there was this intense pain in my stomach. My mouth was burning and I felt dizzy and nauseous. I know I fell and warned you, but I don't remember anything else.'*

'You were poisoned. Dan at the hospital tampered with your blood bags before having someone deliver them to the clinic. The Sheriff is looking for them. The hospital cameras caught him injecting the blood with something. Doc ran tests on samples he took from you and from the other bags. You had four different poisons. Someone was really trying to kill you this time. Tess and Berkley are working on having the wards be able to keep out inanimate objects meant to harm us. It's been a tricky thing to do. They're getting really close though. For now, they extended the ward to the air above the grounds and the earth below too. It's like a huge sphere around the estate. I think they said it's a mile in either direction, but there was talk of that being overkill, so I'm not sure where it ended up. They also put up a ward over the brewery. Berkley's store and the clinic got updated wards as well.'

'I can't think of anyone besides my father who would want to kill me that badly. I never saw Dan, so I can't say if I know him or not. He always seemed to be gone when I would stop over at the hospital.

'Can I please get this catheter out? It's not the most comfortable thing to wear.' Rolf pleaded.

'Your muscles are going to be weak from the poisons and from lying in bed for a week. I don't know if I can get you to the bathroom and back.'

'I'll pee in a bottle. Please?'

Shaye felt through their bond. Rolf was scared that he had almost died and he wanted to feel a little more normal. She sighed. "Fine. Let me wash my hands and grab some gloves. It's going to be uncomfortable, but try to relax."

Rolf grunted as the catheter came out. *'You know, I*

never thought there would be a time when your hands on my penis didn't feel good. I guess I was wrong.'

Shaye laughed at him. "Hey now! I was very gentle." She poured a bottle of water out into a cup for him. "Here is your first empty bottle. Even though you were mean, I'll help if you need me to."

'Can I get the IV out?'

"Nope. That one you are going to have to wait for Doc to okay."

'Okay, love. I'm so tired. I wasn't even up for twenty minutes yet.'

"Rest. I'll give everyone a call and let them know you woke up. They've all been so worried. The guys moved in here when it happened. Not Doc, he still lives at his own house," Shaye clarified. She curled up next to him, rubbing his chest. "Sleep, I'll watch over you."

Seconds later Rolf was asleep again, but it looked like a more natural sleep, not the pain and poison driven unconscious sleep from before. She just lay there for a few minutes, thanking the universe that he came back to her.

Tess poked her head in the room. "Are you okay? I thought I heard you talking?"

"He woke up!" Shaye exclaimed. She wanted to shout but kept it quiet so she wouldn't wake him.

"Seriously?" Tess was so excited she was bouncing on her toes. "I'm going to call Sam!" she said as she ran out of the room.

"I'll call Doc and Berkley," Shaye whisper-shouted after her.

She sighed, feeling finally settled now that he had woken up for even just a few minutes. Grabbing her phone, she called Berkley first to let him know the news. He said he was going to close the shop up early and grab some dinner for everyone, some broth and easy to eat things for Rolf. Doc was also thrilled that his patient was on the mend. He was going to come as soon as his last scheduled patient left for the day and would bring more bagged blood. Now that Rolf was awake, he would need to drink more to build his strength back up.

That evening, there was a mini party in their bedroom. Everyone was in high spirits, giddy with the relief that Rolf had woken up. He still had muscle aches and weakness, but hopefully those would mend soon. Dr. T checked on his patient and stayed for a little while, making sure that Rolf was able to keep down the broth and blood. Rolf managed to convince him to take the IV out, so long as he promised to follow Doc's strict eating and drinking schedule. He was only to drink out of Berkley's mug to help with the healing process. Tess brought a few more healing crystals to place under his pillow. Berkley had made him a pendant that would glow when danger was near.

"I didn't think you would need one of these, since you can sense other paranormals, but clearly I wasn't thinking on a wide enough scale. I made one for all of us and added to the magic already on Shaye's. Even Doc's got one now. Is there anything you need us to help you with?" Berkley asked.

"I would love to make it to the bathroom. Maybe even a shower," Rolf said longingly.

"Berkley and I can help you into the bathroom and I can help him in the shower," Sam volunteered. "Look, I got my swimmies on," he joked, although he did indeed have his bathing suit on. How had none of them noticed that before? "Do you want to strip down here or in the bathroom? Everyone already saw my ass, so it's only fair if you want to show yours off too." Sam was so relieved that his friend was awake and wanted to lighten the mood for everyone.

"Why did everyone see your ass?" Rolf asked, resigning himself to a story.

"Well, some idiot let himself get poisoned and spilled blood all over the floor. I was trying to figure out why it smelled off and had a wee taste. Oh, I was a wolf at the time. It was nasty and I wanted to wash it off my tongue; of course I needed to change back so I could use my hands to turn on the faucet. You know I don't magically keep my clothes on when I change; so clearly, I was naked when I got back into my human form. Don't worry, it was just the butt. Berkley made me put on pants. They were yours, but I'm keeping them now."

Rolf laughed before groaning. "Since your bare dick was on them, you can keep them. Are you okay? The poison didn't hurt you?"

"No, Shaye fixed me up," Sam answered seriously. "I'm so glad you're awake. Come on big guy, let's get you clean. I'm surprised your mate was hugging you. You stink." Sam wrinkled his nose as he and Berkley helped Rolf shuffle into the bathroom.

"Doc brought a shower stool yesterday, so there is someplace for him to sit, just make sure he doesn't fall," Shaye cautioned. "Rolf, let the warm water help relax your muscles. We'll try the shower for now. After you eat and drink, maybe we can try the bathtub later tonight or tomorrow. Some Epsom salts might help with the muscle ache. Oh, and brush your teeth! They're really bad." She laughed.

While Sam made sure Rolf didn't fall in the shower, Berkley grabbed some soft sweatpants and a t-shirt from their closet. Shaye started stripping the used sheets from the bed. Tess grabbed new sheets and helped remake the bed. "There's nothing quite like getting into a bed with brand-new clean sheets," Tess commented. "I'm sure it's going to feel good to get washed off and into a clean bed.

Once the guys get him back in here, we'll get out of your hair. I'm sure this is going to exhaust him."

Shaye nodded. "You guys aren't *leaving* leaving yet, are you?" She had gotten so used to all of them in the house. It was nice to have her family close.

"No, heifer," Tess shot back as she hip-checked her. "You're stuck with me now. I want to live in your hammock pavilion and have nights by the fire. I love having our little family all in one house. It's where I think we're supposed to be. Sam and I already talked about it. We're still going to keep the apartment for us at the brewery, but it will be for date nights or when I want to work someplace besides the house. I'm pretty sure Berkley feels the same. He could use his store's apartment as storage or additional workspace. His stuff is getting noticed and really popular, so I have a feeling that he will need the additional room for the store."

"I love you guys," Shay sniffed as she gave her best friend a hug. "I am so glad I moved here."

They heard the shower shut off. Tess told Shaye that she would run downstairs and get another cup of broth and a mug of blood for Rolf. Shaye turned down the sheets on Rolf's side of the bed. *'Being this weak sucks, love.'* She heard him complain as the guys helped him shuffle slowly back to bed.

'I know,' she responded. *'Tess is bringing up some more for you to drink. I can't wait to hold you,'* she confessed.

After they got him in bed and gave Shaye his drinks, everyone traded hugs as their friends left the room.

"Hold on, Berkley!" Shaye called out.

Walking over to the door, she looked up at her friend. "Thank you for dinner. I also wanted to let you know that you are welcome to stay here as long as you want, forever even. Tess told me that they were going to stay here and just use their apartment for date days or an extra work location. She thought you might want to turn the living space at the store into extra storage or a larger workspace. Either way, you'll always be welcome here," she added.

"Thanks, Shaye. I've loved being here. If it's alright with Rolf, I wouldn't mind moving some of my things over. We can talk about it later when Rolf is up to it." Berkley headed down to the room he had been staying in.

Shaye closed their door, eager to simply snuggle up next to her mate. Rolf was drinking his broth, the blood already finished. He was already looking a little better, exhausted but the shower had clearly woken him up a little bit. *How long is this weakness supposed to last?* he asked.

"If you were human, and had just one of the poisons, then it could last for several weeks. You're a vampire and you heal much faster, but you were also dosed with multiple poisons, so we're not sure. Just stay on Doc's schedule and let me keep working to heal you. Now, lie down so I can snuggle you," Shaye ordered.

That sounds good. Rolf rolled to his side, the little spoon for a change. *I missed you, Mate. Even when I couldn't wake up, I knew you were missing.*

I'm here, I won't leave you. When you're better, let's talk about me turning. This life can be so short. I don't want to miss any of it with you. I want to be able to help protect you too; I can't do that as a human.

Oh, love. You will always have me. I don't want you to rush and regret it, Rolf replied, but he was cautiously hopeful. A thousand plus years with his love seemed perfect. Forever would be grand, but he would take their thousand (ish) years.

"Shit. You should drop a quick thought to your mom too. She called your phone frantic when you were unconscious. I sent her text updates, but I'm sure she would love to know you're awake," Shaye said aloud.

'I guess I can,' he pouted. *'I wanted to snuggle.'*

'I will still snuggle you. Just let her know you're alive, you're up, and that you'll talk to her more tomorrow.'

Shaye held Rolf, grateful he was on the mend. She could tell when he fell asleep, his entire body relaxing. He had been so tense with muscle aches and pains. Now she could try to speed along his healing. Healing always worked better when the person was relaxed. Sighing, she kept one hand on Rolf and reached over to grab his phone where it was beeping on the nightstand with the other. There was a text message from his mom. "Shaye, welcome to the family. I always wanted a daughter. After Rolf changes you and you are comfortable, I will come for a visit. Vlad has hurt my baby too many times. I want to be there to help you defeat him. Love, Mom." On one hand, it was nice to be wanted, to have a mom figure in her life. On the other hand, "defeat him"? Was Rolf planning something already? She would have a talk with him when he woke up, she thought as she started to fall asleep.

Rolf was able to walk to the bathroom on his own in the morning. He still felt weak, but better than yesterday. His eyes were a little sensitive to bright lights and he got dizzy if he stood up too quickly. He managed to eat some oatmeal and a mug of blood for breakfast. Shaye did another healing session on him and the dizziness seemed to be gone. It was progress, slow, but still progress. He was stir-crazy by Saturday afternoon. When Shaye left the bedroom to grab some lunch, he decided to join everyone downstairs. *'I'll be there in a minute, love,'* he told her. *'Don't bring it upstairs,'* he finished as he teleported to the living room. Luckily, he placed himself right in front of the couch so he could sit down. That had tired him, but he was so grateful to be out of the bedroom that he didn't care.

"Are you kidding me right now?" Shaye asked angrily. "You are still healing. First you're making battle plans with your mom, and now you're just teleporting willy-nilly."

"It wasn't willy-nilly. I really needed out of the bedroom. I'm just grateful we moved to your bedroom once the wards were up. I would have been incredibly miserable in my old basement room. Secondly, I didn't make any "battle plans" with my mother. We just both agreed that father will not stop until I'm dead and that we're going to have to fight him sooner or later."

Shaye just huffed and went back into the kitchen. She just got him back from almost dying and he was talking about fighting his pyscho of a dad.

"He's not wrong," Tess said quietly. "I know it's not what you want to hear, especially with everything that happened, but it does seem that his dad won't stop. At this point, it's hard to tell where he might attack from because he is using other people. It seems likely that Dan was working for, or with, Vlad."

"If we can get ahead of him, instead of having to react, we can take him down and then we'll have some peace around here," Sam added. "We have several friends we can call in and have them join us. Even if Vlad has some minions, we have a lot more support between our families, friends, and even the town."

Tess nodded. "I think I can help with the plan. I've been having some dreams lately. Not full dreams, more like snippets. I know which friends to call in and my family will help too. I think it's going to happen here and my family can cast a spell to help protect the town, to make sure the humans don't get caught up in the fight.

Rolfston's mom will be here. There are a few unknowns, people I don't recognize, but they come to help us. We might have a few injuries, but I can't SEE any of us dying if we get this right. In all the scenarios that are good for us, you've already turned though, Shaye."

"I was planning on it when Rolf is back to a hundred percent. I'd hate to take more time off from work, I've barely been there since I started."

Berkley came in from the backyard. "What's going on?" he asked startled. "Is Rolf alright?"

"Everyone is fine," Sam replied.

"Rolf is already thinking of going on the offensive and Shaye was a little angry with him. We're talking about why it will be more of a benefit to us if we get ahead of Vlad."

"I can see that," Berkley said and nodded. "I can put the word out among the Fae when we know a timeframe. Vlad's pissed off a bunch of people, some of whom I think will come to help stop him."

"I think it's time to call Ian and tell him to come home," Tess stated.

"Ian? Why? I don't want him caught up in this mess either," Shaye said. "It's getting dangerous, and I don't want anyone else hurt. Rolf has already been hurt twice by his father, and this last time I didn't know if he would make it. Ian is human, he doesn't need to be anywhere near here. I don't want any other humans in this fight. Even if they are gifted, they won't be strong enough to fight a vampire or werewolf."

"Seriously?" Tess muttered, smacking herself in the forehead. "Ian must have been rather remote not to hear you had mated to a vampire. I would have thought he would have made his way here by now. He's a vampire too, although I'm not sure how old he is. We've never talked about it, but just like when I met Rolf, I can sense it and they can sense me. And no, I didn't mean to keep it a secret from you. I thought he may have told you by now. It's not really my place to out him, so to speak, but I think we need him here," Tess apologized. "All my dreams show him here, he's family. I mean, you've known him for ten years now?"

"Fifteen. His parents moved into the house next to ours during sophomore year of high school. We moved to New Orleans together for college. If he is that much older than me, I'm going to smack him for not telling me sooner. It would explain why he's only been available for phone calls lately. Even during video calls, he will flip the screen around to show me what he's been working on, or where he's at, instead of his face. That pain in my ass. He's definitely getting smacked. I'll give him a call tonight. I need to catch him up on things too. Of course, I hid stuff too, thinking he was human. I need to yell at someone anyway, so he'll do. I can't yell at Rolf, he's too weak, it makes me feel bad," she laughingly said. Her world just kept on changing.

"Who are you going to yell at?" Rolf asked, leaning against the doorway.

"You for not staying on the couch," Tess teased.

"My friend Ian. Apparently, he's a vampire and didn't tell me. He's my oldest friend, based on human years of knowing him at least, so that punk gets to be yelled at. Now get back on the couch and I'll bring you lunch."

"Yes, ma'am," Rolf replied.

Rolf still had some energy left, so Berkley brought out his *Ticket To Ride* game. He'd been saving it for when Rolf felt better. Tess crushed it the first round. Doc stopped over to check on Rolf and was happy with his progress. He encouraged him to stick to the feeding schedule until he was back to one hundred percent, then he could go back to his monthly feedings.

"Once you are completely recovered, then you can turn Shaye, but not before. It would be too hard on both of you. I'll have more blood on standby as well," he told Rolf.

"I don't want to keep you short-staffed, Doc. I feel like a horrible employee," Shaye confessed.

Tess spoke up. "If Rolf keeps recovering well, you can go back on Monday and I'll work from home so someone is with Rolf. I've been doing medical coding because it's easy to do remotely and I know the medical field. I've kept my nursing license up to date and am licensed to practice here. I had no idea why I wanted to take the test for Tennessee, but I did it a couple of years ago. While you turn, I can step in, so Doc isn't short-staffed while you're out," she said, looking at Doc for confirmation.

Doc nodded. "Sounds like a good plan to me."

"Sit down, Doc. I'm going to go make dinner, you can take over my color," Shaye said.

It turned out Doc was secretly addicted to *Ticket To Ride*, although he played on the app normally. He won by a landslide, completing all his routes and getting longest route. He even showed them how far he had gotten in his garden in *Gardenscapes*. Doc was finally starting to loosen up around them, Shaye thought fondly. She was glad; it didn't seem like Doc had anyone he was really close to in town. He was such a nice guy and she was glad she could fold him into her family.

Rolf went back to bed after dinner. After making sure he was settled, Shaye went back downstairs to call Ian so that she wouldn't wake Rolf. Curling up in her favorite oversized chair in the library, she took a deep breath and hit the call button. It took a few rings before she heard Ian's sleepy accented voice.

"Hullo?"

"Hey, Freckles. How are you? Where are you now?"

"Shaye? How are ye, ma wee bony lass?"

"Don't even try to butter me up. Why didn't you tell me, Ian?"

"I dinnae ken whit ye are going on aboot," he replied.

"Okay. I'll give you a minute to wake up. Your brogue is always stronger when you just wake up. And then you and I are going to have a little talk."

"Coffee first," Ian agreed, stumbling to find his Keurig.

After a few bracing gulps, Ian was a little more coherent. "What's up?"

"Can I just say, it's always been weird how you switch from a Scottish brogue to barely having an accent at all. I guess it makes sense when you're so old."

"Old? Who are you calling old? Do you see any wrinkles yet? Hmm?"

"Well, I've heard that about vampires. They don't seem to age much between twenty-five and eighteen hundred years old," Shaye casually mentioned.

"What?" Ian shouted. "When did you...how did you...?" he sputtered.

"Yup, I've learned all kinds of things lately. My mate's a vampire, apparently Tess is a witch, and now I'm friends with a Fae and a werewolf. My mate's dad is trying to kill him, that's how I met him. Rolf just woke up yesterday after he was poisoned and was unconscious for a week. Oh, and once he's better, I'm taking more time off from the clinic I'm working at and turning." She paused for a breath. She just kind of word vomited everything. She may have overwhelmed Ian, as she heard only silence for a full minute. She looked down at her phone to make sure they hadn't been disconnected.

"Hello?" she asked. "You still there?"

"That's a lot to unpack, lass. Go slower and tell me the whole story," Ian instructed.

Shaye wandered into the kitchen to grab her own cup of coffee. She tried to tell Ian the most important parts of the story, starting with how she met Rolf and ending with how her mate and friends want to make a stand.

"Weel, you've had an exciting month, haven't ye? How old is your mate? And did you say Vladimir?"

"Yes. He's around two hundred. How old are you?"

"I'm a wee bit younger; one hundred and fifty. Are you okay wi' turning, he's no' pressuring you, is he? How are your powers right now? It sounds like you've been using them a lot," Ian asked, concerned.

"Well, you're still a lot older than me, old man. No, Rolf has been great. He told me from the beginning that he would do whatever I wanted, that we could wait to mate, mate without turning, or do both. He just wants me to be happy. I have been using the healing a lot more recently with how much Rolf has been injured. Berkley gave me magical coffee mugs that help with my energy levels and a pendant for magical protection. Tess gave me a crystal satchel when I was healing Rolf this last time. I have it upstairs and will bring it into work when I go back on Monday; it seemed to make a big difference. The house and grounds, as well as the clinic and the guys' shops, are warded so it should be safe.

"Tess might call you too. She thought you would have heard that I had mated, somehow. She wants you to come home. So do I, but it might be dangerous right now," Shaye added.

"I've been traveling wi' a human-run Renaissance Festival group and hae no' seen any other vampires in a while. Give me a minute…Rolf's your mate and Vladimir is his father… Shite!" he exclaimed. "Crazy Vlad is your new father-in-law. How did you find yourself in this situation? Every vampire knows of Vlad; Tess is right, I'm sure it will spread through the gossip rounds like wildfire that Rolf has mated. Vlad is getting old and has been trying to control as much of the world as he can. From what I heard, Rolf won't join wi' his da' and that infuriates Vlad. He wants to collect power and use it for his own. As much as you don't want it, they're right about bringing the fight on your own terms. Let me finish up this tour, I have a few weeks left and I'll head your way. I'll stand wi' you, just let me know when you have a plan. If you need me sooner, call. I can be there quickly. I'll spread the word to a few others that I know," Ian promised.

"Will you come to stay?" Shaye asked.

"You really want me to stay with you? Do ye have the room?" Ian asked. Shaye could tell he was more awake. His accent was not as strong and he was fluctuating between using it and not.

"Yes, to both. The house definitely has enough room. The town has a few buildings available if you wanted to work here instead of traveling all the time, although we could probably make a forge area/workshop on the grounds too," Shaye enticed.

"Aye, I'll come home. I've missed my wee lass. If Rolf won't mind, I can easily do my metal and leather work there. I would just need to build a new forge. I've been focused on the leatherwork lately but would love to get back to the metal."

"You're family. He won't mind," Shaye assured him.

"Get some sleep, *piuthar*. I'll see you soon," he vowed.

Shaye felt a little more at ease. Her friend was coming home, and he'd just called her "sister." He had always been like a big brother. She couldn't wait to see him. She would just have to trust in Tess's visions and their friends' collective wisdom. They hadn't led her wrong yet. Turning off the lights and double-checking the locks, she headed upstairs to sleep next to her mate.

10

It was finally the day. Rolf was completely recovered, although Shaye discovered that injured vampires were the worst patients. At least humans stayed put while healing for the most part, they didn't try to teleport places because they were "bored." Even with the moonstone removed, the crystal satchel really did help Shaye not use as much of her energy while healing at the clinic. Sam and Berkley had moved most of their things into the rooms they had picked out. Berkley was trying to figure out how he wanted to renovate his store to make the most of the now empty space. They had had a nice relaxing day of eating her favorite foods and relaxing with their friends for her birthday. Rolf had surprised her with a ring. He wanted to show her he loved her in both of their cultures.

They had made a loose plan of her turning and preparing to confront Vlad. Very few people would know when she actually turned. The idea was to spread the word that she and Rolf were having a commitment ceremony, followed by her turning. They were hoping it would look like a party with their friends and family and that Vlad, thinking that they were distracted, would attack then. Tess had already gotten familiar with the clinic and had been alternating days with her for a few weeks, but never in a recognizable pattern. Doc had given them additional blood to have on hand at the house for her turning. He sourced it from a few different hospitals in surrounding towns instead of just the local hospital, spacing it out as well so that it didn't draw any more attention.

Ian was almost done with his last festival and would be here in a week or two. Word had been sent to their friends that they could use their help, if they were willing.

All good things, but she was still a big ball of nerves this morning. She couldn't sleep much last night. She knew she wanted to turn, to be more robust so that she could help keep her mate and friends safe in the upcoming fight, to spend years with her family. She was still worried about her healing becoming even more over-whelming once she turned, but Berkley's and Tess's gifts had already helped a lot, so she was hopeful that would continue. Right now, she was enjoying her cup of coffee and watching the sunrise. She would turn tonight and Tess would cover at the clinic tomorrow, Monday. She was hopeful that her turning was quick and that she would have good control over herself when she woke up. She wanted this business with Vlad over by Thanksgiving so that she could celebrate the holiday for the first time since college with her two best friends and her new family without worrying. She would have to make sure to invite Doc too.

Rolf joined her at the window. "Morning, love," he said as he wrapped his arms around her from behind, giving her neck a kiss. "We can wait. You don't have to do this if you've changed your mind."

"Just nervous," she replied, leaning back into him. "Besides, Tess said I had changed in her dreams. This is the right path; I just don't like the unknowns. Is anyone else up yet?"

"Berkley ran to his shop. He had an order to ship out. Sam and Tess are up, but I don't think they're coming out for breakfast for a while. I'll set aside some bacon for them."

"Why—oh." Shaye laughed. She enjoyed lazy Sunday mornings in bed too.

Everyone was back at the house by lunchtime, even Doc. It was warm out for the beginning of November, so Rolf made a fire in the outdoor fireplace, and they all hung out in the hammocks and lounge chairs. Shaye ran inside to get the items for s'mores and to make some hot chocolates for everyone.

The rest of the group went out to dinner to give them some privacy. Rolf led her upstairs to their bathroom, where he had a bath waiting for her. Candles were lit and there was soft music playing. He undressed her slowly, kissing his way down her body, paying attention to her hot spots. The curve of her neck, her inner wrist, behind her knees, all of those spots got little nibbles and soft kisses, but he teased her by completely ignored her pussy. Her lips were nice and plump, she could feel how wet she was, but he still didn't touch her there. Rolf gently took her hair down and massaged her scalp for a minute, her muscles relaxing under his care. He held out a hand and helped her into the tub, climbing in behind her. She let her head fall back against his chest as he traced a path down her body with his finger, still avoiding her wet heat. Shaye turned her head, silently asking for a kiss.

Rolf plunged his tongue into her mouth, twisting his tongue around hers. Grabbing her hair, he urged her to turn around. Shaye straddled his lap, his cock riding between the crease of her ass. His tongue was teasing hers, taking a deep kiss and then retreating into little pecks. Letting go of her hair, Rolf grabbed her cheeks, pulling her tight against him. He licked her nipples, lightly sucking them, then switched to kissing her neck. Shaye was starting to rock against him, seeking out friction on her clit. He reached down a hand, sliding a finger between her lips and finding her bud. Rubbing it gently at first, he applied more pressure as he took a little sip from her neck. Shaye climaxed instantly; he could feel her vagina getting even wetter for him.

"Time to get out of the bath, love," he said as he lifted her out. He grabbed a couple towels from the rack and carried her into the bedroom. Laying one towel down on the bed first, he laid her down. "Let me dry you off, Mate," he teased as he started licking down her body.

Shaye laughed. "I don't think that's working," she said. "I'm still pretty wet."

"Here?" he asked, rubbing the towel over her breasts, loving how her breath hitched.

"Lower," she gasped. The towel gently rubbed down her body to her stomach.

"Here?"

"Lower." She laughed breathlessly.

"Here?" he asked as he dried off her legs.

"No, higher," she demanded, spreading her legs.

He moaned seeing her glistening lips. He couldn't wait to taste her. She smelled delightful. "Ah, I think I see it. Here?" he asked, barely touching her skin.

Shaye loved the feel of the cotton against her skin, it could be so soft and yet a little rough with the right amount of pressure. "Harder please, Mate. I need more to come again."

She watched as Rolf wrapped the towel around his finger. He bent his head and spreading her lips, he gently lapped at her arousal. Her clit was engorged, waiting for pleasure. He teased her a bit, lightly licking, tracing patterns with his tongue. Soon she was squirming, desperate for a firmer touch. The light touches felt amazing, but her orgasm was always just out of reach. She wanted to be filled, wanted to feel his hard cock rubbing against her walls, hitting her G-spot. "Harder, Mate, and then fill me. I want to feel full." She screamed as Rolf used the finger wrapped in the towel to give her the friction she needed against her clit. The pressure and the roughness sent sparks of pleasure shooting through her body. She felt incredibly floaty as she came back from her orgasm.

'Fill me up, Mate. Make me yours forever,' Shaye told him, her hands pulling him up her body.

Rolf crawled up her body, leaning down to kiss her. *'I love you, Mate,'* he said as he slid into her welcoming body. She was so warm and wet, her cunt grabbing onto him, squeezing him tight. Working his knees farther forward, he put her ass up at an angle. As her legs wrapped around his waist, he pounded into her, setting a fast and hard rhythm guaranteed to graze over all her sensitive nerve endings. He reached down with one hand, rubbing small circles on her clit. He could feel his balls drawing up tight and knew his own orgasm was close. *'Ready, love?'* he asked.

'Turn me, Mate. I love you,' Shaye answered, turning her head so he could bite her.

Leaning down, he licked over her neck, making her shiver, and slid his teeth gently into her skin. Her blood rushed over his tongue, sweet and spicy just like his love. Shaye gasped again as another orgasm rushed through her. He kept his teeth in her, envisioning her turning. When enough time had passed, he pulled his fangs out. Cutting a spot on his own wrist with his fangs, he held it over her mouth. *'Drink, love. I'll be here when you wake up.'* His own orgasm barreled through him as he felt the pull of her mouth against his skin drinking. When she fell asleep, he pulled his wrist away and gently withdrew from her warmth.

He ran into the bathroom to grab a warm washcloth to wipe her clean. She had a few drops of blood near her mouth and his seed was leaking from her body. That wouldn't be comfortable to wake up to, he thought. Once she was clean, he folded down the sheets, picked her up, laid her down gently, and covered her with the blankets. He could sense the changes slowly happening through their bond.

Rolf grabbed his phone and sent out a group text to their friends, "You can come home now. She's resting."

It had been four days. Four very long days and Shaye had not woken up yet. Rolf was pacing in the front entry, waiting for Doc to arrive to check on Shaye. He felt her through their bond, but he didn't know why she hadn't woken up yet. Today, Tess had gone to the clinic with her hair hidden and dressed in Shaye's clothes. Berkley had stopped at the brewery to pick up Shaye's favorite lunch and brought it over to the clinic. If someone looked too closely, they would see the difference, but they were hoping that someone was just observing from far away and would assume it was Shaye going into work. Doc only took in trusted patients to see Tess, all others he saw himself, saying his nurse was busy in another room if anyone asked. Even Sherri, their human receptionist, made a couple of phone calls back to the break room to give "Shaye" a message from Rolf.

His mother had finished packing up her most important things and had them shipped over this morning. She had a suitcase full of things for when she came over herself, which was supposed to be in two days. She thought Shaye might want to have a female vampire to talk to. Personally, Rolf thought she just couldn't wait to meet Shaye and to gain a daughter.

The doorbell rang and he rushed to get it. He stood there. There was a short person on the front steps looking up at him with blue eyes identical to his and curly black hair pulled into a ponytail. There was an enormous suitcase next to her.

"Are you going to let me in?" his mother asked, looking up at him. "It's a little chilly out here."

"Mother, what are you doing here? I thought you weren't coming for another couple of days?"

"I couldn't wait. I'm so excited to meet her!" His mother practically bounced. "Where's my hug? Aren't you glad to see me?"

"Yes, of course I'm glad to see you! I was just surprised," he said as he picked her up in a hug.

Emma laughed and squeezed her son tight. "Now put me down before anyone sees me being silly."

"We're all a little silly around here," Berkley said behind them. "Sam's pulling Shaye's car into the garage. She had a bit of a headache, so he drove home. Doc's coming right behind us."

"Let's head inside, Mom, and we can talk."

After shutting the door, he made sure the curtains were drawn. "What's going on?" his mother asked.

"Shaye hasn't woken up yet. Tess went into work pretending to be Shaye, just in case Vlad has someone watching the clinic. We're trying to keep to the original plan."

"Did I mess up by coming early?" Emma asked, worried.

"No, Rolf could use someone to pace with during the day while we're at work," Tess teased as she came into the room. "I'm going to go change and I'll come back to start on dinner."

"I put a white chicken chili in the slow cooker this morning," Rolf said. "It should be ready whenever we want to eat."

"I can go make corn muffins to go with it," his mother offered, already walking to the kitchen. She had already seen the whole house at one point or another during their video calls. A lot of them had happened when Rolf was cooking, so she knew where some things were already.

"I can help," Sam offered.

Hearing another knock on the door, Berkley said he would go let Doc in. After saying hello to the room, Doc laid his coat on a chair. "Hey, Doc, thanks for coming over. Do you want to stay for dinner? I have chicken chili in the slow cooker. I've heard rumors of corn muffins too," Rolf offered.

"They'll be ready soon," Emma shouted from the kitchen.

"My mother arrived a couple of days early as a surprise," Rolf told Doc.

"I would love to stay for dinner," Doc replied. He was tickled that they kept including him. He had been getting lonely, but this group just adopted him into their fold. He nodded at them all and headed upstairs to check on Shaye, Rolf just a step behind him.

Looking over Shaye, he couldn't find a reason that she hadn't woken up yet. All her vitals were stable, he could sense the change was finished, she just wasn't ready to wake up yet. "She looks healthy. The change is complete, so she should wake up at any moment. Maybe the next time you have a drink, make sure it's nice and warm to help enhance the scent and drink it in here. It might entice her to wake up if she's hungry. Let me change out her saline bag, and I'll be right down for dinner." After Rolf left the room, Doc sent a push of his own healing energy into her, just to make sure she woke up. If he ever had a daughter, he would want it to be Shaye. He felt like the father of the whole group of youngsters in this house. Youngsters, he snorted to himself. Some days he felt old.

Rolf took a deep breath as he came downstairs. The scent of the chili and the corn muffins was making his stomach rumble. He felt a little relieved that Doc confirmed Shaye's turning had completed successfully.

"Rolf, can I talk to you a minute?" His mom rushed over to him a little frantic.

"Is everything okay? What's wrong?"

'Do you smell that?' she asked quietly in his mind.

'I don't smell anything different here, other than dinner,' Rolf said, confused. He took a deep breath to make sure he wasn't missing something.

'Mom, I don't know what you smell. I don't sense anything different,' he said worriedly. Her sense of smell usually wasn't that much better than a human's, so he wasn't sure what she was picking up on.

'It's faint, but I smelled it in here. I just haven't figured where it's coming from,' Emma replied.

'Let's take a walk around the room, then and try to figure it out. I'll see if I notice anything different.'

When they reached the front door, she stopped abruptly by the chair. "Here!" she said excitedly.

"Mom, there's nothing here but Doc's coat. Oh… You haven't met Dr. T yet, have you?" Rolf asked. "He owns a clinic in town and treats humans and paranormals. Shaye works there as a nurse. He's been here forever, but I'm not sure what kind of paranormal he is. Doc is a great guy," he encouraged her.

"Rolfston, while I'm glad you like your doctor, I'm not

sure what that has to do with the smell." Emma was getting frustrated.

"Mom. Think. You noticed one smell above all the others here…" He led her to the answer.

"Crap." Emma sighed. "I have a mate?" She switched to speaking mentally to her son. *'I never wanted a mate after your father. You know I get skittish around men sometimes. Maybe I can leave until he goes home, and I can come meet Shaye later?'* she asked hopefully.

'If it were me, what would you tell me, Mom?' Rolf asked. He was secretly pleased his mom had finally found a mate and that he was someone Rolf knew and trusted.

'To trust in Fate and give him a chance,' she grumbled.

"Exactly. He really is a good guy. I'm pleased with who Fate picked for you. Now, just remember to give him a chance," he ordered as he heard footsteps coming downstairs.

"Hey, Doc. Have you met my mother yet?" Rolf asked innocently. Inside, his inner child was doing a happy dance for his mom.

"No, I have not had the pleasure," Doc replied, coming over to shake Emma's hand. He froze as soon as their hands touched. "Mate?" he asked softly.

"Mate," Emma confirmed shakily. "I need to take it slowly though," she admitted.

"That is perfectly acceptable. I would love a chance to court you," Doc replied. "My name is Albert." Rolf just kind of stared at Doc. They had always known him as Dr. T or Doc.

"Emmaline, but I usually go by Emma," she replied as Doc kissed the back of her hand.

Tess came running down the stairs. "Hey, what did I miss?"

"Shaye is healthy, still sleeping. Mom and Doc are mates," Rolf responded.

Tess's squeal probably made poor Sam's ears bleed, Rolf thought to himself dryly. The noise brought Sam and Berkley out from the kitchen. "Congratulations," they told the newly discovered mates.

"The muffins are done," Berkley added. "If everyone wants to sit, I can start bringing things out."

Doc held out his arm for Emma and pulled out her chair when they reached the table.

Dinner turned out well, Rolf thought to himself. Everyone was busy eating and talking about their day. Doc was slowly getting Emma to come out of her shell. Almost all his family was under one roof, though there were a few friends who had become like brothers over the years that weren't here. Yet. He had plans to try to get them to come and stay. The town was friendly to paranormals, and it was a safe place; well, it would be safer once they got rid of his father.

"Something smells good," they heard someone say. "Is there still some left?" Everyone gasped and turned around. Shaye was standing casually in the doorway.

"You're awake!" Rolf rushed toward her. He lifted his mate into his arms, holding her tight, his face buried in her neck. He could feel tears of relief prickling in his eyes. *'Love, I missed you. I am so happy you came back to me. I was worried when you didn't wake up sooner.'* He heard everyone go hide in the kitchen to give them some privacy. Well, as much privacy as you can have with a group of paranormals with enhanced hearing.

'Well, give me a kiss then. I brushed my teeth,' Shaye replied with a smile. She was so happy to be holding her mate.

'How do you feel, love?'

'Good. Hungry, a little thirsty. I could probably use a shower too, but the chili smelled so good,' Shaye responded.

'Just to warn you…my mother came early. She came today.

She met Doc a few minutes ago. They're mates. Can you believe it? And Doc's name is Albert, which I never would have guessed. He doesn't seem like an Albert to me.'

'*I guess you better introduce me to your mom then. Do I look okay? Should I go change?*' Shaye asked worriedly. She had been so focused on the food and Rolf, that she hadn't noticed another person at the table.

"Mom, come meet my mate, Shaye," Rolf called out.

'*Put me down first!*' Shaye scolded.

"Hi, Emma. It's nice to finally meet you," Shaye said.

"Shaye, let me give you a hug. I am so excited to meet my new daughter," Emma said, wrapping Shaye up in the first motherly hug she had had since she was a small child. Both of them had tears in their eyes when the hug ended.

Tess pounced on Shaye next. "Hey, lady. Welcome to being a paranormal," Tess said as she gave her a hug too.

Sam and Berkley each took their own turns hugging their friend.

"Are you hungry?" Doc asked after his own hug.

"The chili smells great. I would love a corn muffin," Shaye said as she looked toward the kitchen. "You guys go back to eating, I don't want to interrupt. I'll come join you in a minute."

"I meant more like blood," Doc clarified. "Do we smell tasty?" he teased. He also wanted to know. After first waking up, most vampires were extremely thirsty. With guidance and a mentor, they all could learn to control it, but when they first woke up, sometimes it was with the self-control of a toddler. Shaye had already been standing there several minutes and had gotten hugs from everyone in the group. At least one of them should have smelled slightly enticing.

"Oh! I guess? I mean, I am, but it's not like I can't

wait. I can have some with dinner, right? Is it weird that I'm not thirstier?" Shaye asked, concerned.

"I think it makes perfect sense," Emma said. "Your body knows it can feed safely from its mate, who is right here, so it's not desperate to hunt and feed. You're in your home with your family, so you know you're safe. Plus, you are a healer, so to cause someone an injury by attacking them for food, is to go against your base nature."

"Sit," Rolf urged his mate. "I'll go get your dinner and drink."

Shaye sat, a little self-consciously. It seemed like her acting like her normal self, wasn't normal. She felt an invisible hug from Rolf. *'I don't think it's that, love. I don't remember really being out of control when I woke, although at the time I thought I was due to my father's deceit. Mom didn't really get out of control either. I think some people just have an easier time with the turn. The ones who struggle tend to get the most attention, so that's what everyone assumes all turns are like,'* Rolf reassured her.

"Here you go, love." Rolf kissed the top of her head as he placed her food down in front of her.

Shaye dug into the chili. The bowl was empty pretty quickly, but she hadn't eaten in several days, so she didn't feel too bad about scarfing it down. Rolf brought her another bowl. Once everyone had started eating their own food again, Shaye looked uncertainly at her mug. The dark liquid smelled good, definitely not like the coppery scent blood used to have when she was human. *'It's okay, Mate. I had some at dinner and so did my mother. No one is paying attention, just have your meal.'* Shaye took a deep breath and quickly swallowed a mouthful. It was a surprising taste. She always laughed at the descriptions on a wine bottle and how seriously the sommeliers were about "hints of oak, peat, blackberry, chocolate, etc." but now she got it. You could taste hints of different flavors in the blood. She finished her cup, as well as her second helping of dinner.

Rolf stood up and held out a hand to Shaye. "Well, thank you all for coming to dinner. Shaye is getting tired, so I'm going to take her up to bed."

'I am?' Shaye asked, laughing.

'Yup, so tired,' Rolf tried to say sternly.

Everyone at the table said goodnight, trying not to smile. Tess waggled her eyebrows at Shaye, humming "Let's Get It On."

Rolf picked her up and ran up the stairs. "You can rest if you want to, but I needed to hold you."

They lay on the bed facing each other, holding hands.

Shaye looked at him nervously. "Can I taste you?" she asked.

Rolf's dick plumped up. "Always," he replied.

Shaye scooted closer and placed her head in the crook of his neck, just breathing him in. His scent had always been appealing, but now it was stronger. There was this spot on his neck where it was the strongest and she licked over it. *'Hmm, there love. Can I bite at the same time?'* Rolf asked.

'Yes, please. That sounds amazing.' Shaye moaned as she bit down and tasted Rolf's blood for the first time. The combination of his blood in her mouth and his teeth sinking into her neck, sent an orgasm rushing through her.

"Wow," she panted. "That was crazy. I've never come that fast."

"Me either," Rolf said ruefully. He had come in his pants like a teenager. The joint feeding had been like a sensory loop between them, amazing and overwhelming.

They drifted off to sleep wrapped around each other.

Rolf sat at the kitchen table going through his contacts. Shaye was doing extremely well as a vampire. It had been a seamless transition once she had woken up. Her natural shields had thankfully been increased when she turned, so that while she still felt others' pain, she could control it much better. Shaye said it was like touching an ice cube with a bare finger and then touching it again with gloves on. She could still feel the sensation, but it was muted and manageable. She went back to work just days after waking up from turning. They were keeping the alternative scheduling with Tess and Shaye both working at the clinic so that her time away didn't seem suspicious. It was time to move forward with the rest of their plan. He had the fake party invitation ready to send out. They were going the electronic route so that it could be easily shared with anyone they may have missed. This was only being sent to their trusted friends, those that would come and stand with them against Vladimir, but they were encouraged to talk about it as they went about their day, especially near other paranormals. Sam's brewery and Berkley's store would also have a sign posted on the front doors that they would be closed that day for a family celebration. He read down the invitation again, making sure the details were correct.

You are cordially invited to the Mating and Turning
celebration of
Rolfston
and
Shaye
Please join us at the estate in Rockfort, Tennessee
On November 12ᵗʰ at 6:00 pm

The brief ceremony will be followed by a celebration lasting
until the wee hours.
The new mates will be in attendance for an hour or so,
but will leave to complete her turning.

**Friends are welcome to stay the night.*
There will be a few supplies available, but please feel free to
bring your own.
Come ready to party.

It's not what he would have had on his real invitation, but he supposed it would do. Taking a deep breath, he hit send on the email. They would have just over a week to get ready for when Vlad came to visit, if he took the bait.

His phone immediately started blowing up with RSVP's. They had all been just waiting for confirmation of the date. Shaye's friend Ian had been held up with some problems at the last Festival, but he would get here just in time. His friend, Gawain, was already on the way. Tess's family group was sending a few of the stronger members to help them and should be here by the end of the week. They wanted to be there early to get a feel for the town and the property. Tess would be working with them to set up protection around the town so that troublemakers would not be allowed to cross the town boundary lines. They had already cleared the plan with the Sheriff and the Mayor. The Sheriff, although a paranormal, would stay in town until the battle was finished to make sure the town was protected. As a Warden, he had granted permission for the plan and for Rolf to take out his father. Vlad was a scourge on paranormals everywhere.

The wards on the house grounds were going to be slightly modified for the one night. There would be an opening in the wards that would allow for an access path that led to a clearing behind the house. The rest of the grounds and house would still be covered. If anyone on their side was injured, they could retreat behind the wards to get help. Doc was going to be stationed at the house for any injuries. After they defeated Vlad, the wards would be restored to normal.

11

The day for their "ceremony" opened with a bright crisp morning. Most everyone was here already, although there were a few still on their way. There was going to be a pow-wow of sorts with the friends and family that were already here with others joining via video call. It would give everyone a chance to unofficially meet and know what their allies would look like.

Gawain had arrived a few days ago. He brought his RV and truck, so he was living on the house grounds. They were able to hook him up to some electric and water, but there weren't any RV sewer hookups on the property, so he was coming into the house for bathroom and shower use. As a falcon shifter, he had been doing flyovers of the land around the town, looking for signs of Vlad and any of his followers. He found a camp a few miles out yesterday. At the time it looked like Vlad had about twenty or so men with him.

Tess, her family members, and Berkley were studying the property and town maps, making sure that all wards were functional and in place. Shaye was nervously pacing. She wasn't used to the violence that could come with being a paranormal. Granted, it had improved greatly through the years, but there were still instances of it. "With great power, comes great responsibility" and all that, but there was always someone who just wanted more power like his father. Shaye was also worried that she hadn't heard from Ian yet. He had left three days ago and should have made it by now. Rolf hoped he arrived soon so that Shaye could stop worrying.

Shaye came running down the stairs. "Ian's here!" she exclaimed.

"I didn't hear the door. How do you know he's here?" Rolf asked.

"I'm not sure. Ever since I woke up, I can sense all of you now. I can feel each of your energies and tell them apart." After dropping that bomb of information, she threw open the door and jumped on the man in front of her. "I'm so happy you finally made it! What took you so long?"

Ian gave her a hug back. "Hi, little sister," he said. "I ran into a couple of Vlad's minions on my way. We just happened to be going to the same place and I had to go around them, so it took me a little longer than I thought it would. I drove this time so that I could bring my equipment and gear. I have some weapons that might be useful; I'm not sure what the plan is, but I made sure to bring all of my fighting quality weapons. If it had been just me, I would have just run here and been here faster."

"What do you mean run?" Rolf asked curiously.

"One of my abilities once I turned, was speed. I run about five times faster than the average vampire. I'm hoping that comes in handy during the battle and I can catch some of them off guard. I managed to park the truck and trailer and scout out their camp. I could see about twenty people, but they did have tents up as well, so I'm not sure on an accurate head count. I think I have maybe ten to fifteen good-quality swords, as well as some daggers. I packed in a hurry, so I'll have to get into the trailer to get an accurate number. I have some leather chest armor in there as well," Ian offered.

Rolf shook his hand. "Welcome to our home. I'm sure what you brought will be incredibly useful. We only had a few things here on the grounds. I know a few people brought their personal equipment, but I know we can always use more."

Just then, Tess came into the room with her family members. "We're all done, wards are set," she announced as she walked through the door. "Ian!" she shouted as she ran over to give him a hug. "I haven't seen you in forever," she said. "Are you going to stick around for a while after today?" she asked with a curious look on her face.

"Yes," he said, "as ye well know, you little minx. Shaye asked me to come home, so I'm here to stay. I might still go out on the Renaissance Festival circuit occasionally just to keep my name out there. I may open a store in town, if I think I can sell enough through the storefront or have enough online sales to pay for it. Rolf also offered to build me a forge in the backyard. It looks like there won't be any shortage of space for me." He laughed. "This place is huge."

Berkley came into the room and Shaye called him over. "Berkley, come meet Ian!"

Ian looked over, his nostrils flaring. "Well, hello there," he purred. "Who do we have here?" he asked coquettishly.

Berkley took Ian's hand, raising it to his lips. "Hello, Mate," he greeted Ian.

"Mates?" Shaye asked excitedly.

"Mates," Ian confirmed, staring at Berkley.

"Berkley, I have all sorts of stories from when Ian was in school with me. Just let me know if you want any of the embarrassing stories. Tess probably has some too," Shaye teased.

Berkley laughed. "I'll take all the stories you have."

Shaye was so pleased. She had always wanted to have a loving family and for her friends to be happy. Now all her closest friends were here, her chosen family, and they had found their mates.

Tess was grinning, winking over at Shaye. It looked like her dreams had been correct so far, and she was so grateful to have everyone nearby. If things kept going to plan, tonight's fight would be successful.

"Mate, would you help me unload some things and then we can go talk?" Ian asked.

"Let's put everything on the back porch for now," Rolf said. "We can all help unload to make things go quicker. That way you will have more time together before we have to get to the gathering place."

With everyone helping, they were able to unload the weapons and armor that Ian had brought. There were swords, daggers, leather armor, and a few chainmail pieces. After everything that was needed for tonight was unloaded, Ian locked his trailer back up. Berkley held out his hand and led Ian inside and up the stairs.

"What's next?" Shaye asked.

"We can go over the loose plan one more time," Tess said, grabbing the property map from the table. "I'll show you where the ward lines stop so that you know where the safety line is. The path to the clearing will be open but will alert us when someone crosses. The protection wards will still cover the back patio and porch area, the house, and the rest of the grounds. Doc will have a medical area set up on the patio, but right now the supplies are hiding in one of the outdoor storage bins by the deck.

"The outdoor meeting/ceremony space is all set up and decorated like it's a party. I didn't go too heavy on setting the scene, since I don't want anything to really get in our way during any fighting. We marked a path from the driveway that has a "This Way To The Celebration" sign and is lined with ribbons. I think Vlad and his cronies will try to just walk right in acting like invited guests. We positioned the ceremony platform so that the patio and house area are behind it; granted there is about thirty feet or so of space between the platform and the patio, but the tiki torches by the patio are marked with ribbons as well. The ribbons will hopefully help mark where the ward boundaries are. Emma and Doc have been in the kitchen getting medical supplies together and making lunch. I think she has several huge slow cookers going for dinner as well," Tess concluded.

"Why don't you all come and eat?" Emma said, poking her head out of the kitchen. "I'll save some for Ian and Berkley when they come down."

It was 5:00 pm and Rolf stood by the front doors pacing and waiting. He had received confirmation that all of the friends who had committed to coming were on the grounds or in town. They had arrived by all different methods: flight, car, walking or running, some by teleporting. The driveway was going to be full, but there was parking available on the street as well. Many had even brought others to help make a stand against Vlad. Since it would have looked too suspicious to have everyone there early, some were hanging out in town until closer to the ceremony. They would be walking up the driveway and using the path. If Vlad was trying to blend in, he would be following their late-arriving guests.

The plan was for most of their guests to be in the clearing about 5:30 pm and he could already see a few of them making their way back there. He would arrive with Ian, Berkley, and Sam at 5:45. Shaye would come with Emma and Tess a few minutes before 6:00. It was a little similar to how a human wedding would run, he thought.

Everyone at the house was getting changed if they needed to and grabbed a weapon if they didn't have one of their own. Of course, most of their friends were older and had their own collection; but they did have a few younger ones who had not grown up in the time where they needed a weapons collection of their own. The witches seemed to rely on magic, so most of them did not have fighting gear of their own. The armor Ian made was able to be worn under clothes for the most part or blended in very well. He had brought Shaye a leather chest armor that fit over her dress to look like a bodice so that she could still wear it to the ceremony and have it blend in. It was a gorgeous piece of work and had a dagger hidden along her back that she could grab. The air was a bit chilly, so people were able to wear cloaks, capes, sweaters, and jackets that helped hide their weapons and armor.

Tess popped her head in. "Everyone is following the schedule. So far it looks good. It's time for you guys to head out. I'm bringing Shaye through the patio so that she is under the ward until the last possible minute. Doc said he put a sign up at the clinic that it would be closed beginning at 6:00, so it doesn't look weird that he isn't at the ceremony yet."

Rolf nodded and took a deep breath. He met with Sam, Berkley, and Ian, and they headed out the front door. They could feel eyes upon them as they walked down the ribbon-lined path off of the driveway, but they kept chatting and joking like they didn't notice anything. He stopped along the way, greeting his guests and made his way to stand on the platform. Standing there, he kept one eye on the crowd while talking to his trio. He knew Gawain was perched in one of the trees in his falcon form so that he could get a better perspective on incoming groups.

Shaye, Tess, and his mom began walking to the platform. Shaye was wearing an off-white knee-length Renaissance-style dress with a loose, flowing skirt that was slightly longer in the back. The sleeves were also loose and reached down to her wrists. The black battle armor looked like a bodice or corset, emphasizing her waist. Her wavy brown hair was loose, save for a braid on either side that formed a crown. The pendant from Berkley was prominently displayed and already glowing. He knew that he had to keep his guards up, as there was danger nearby, but Shaye was absolutely breathtaking.

Once they reached the platform, his mother stepped in front of them. "Thank you, everyone, for coming to see my only son, Rolfston, and my new daughter-in-law Shaye's Mating Ceremony. I am so excited for her to join our family. As you may know, she helped save Rolfston's life twice recently. We are pleased that she has decided to not only join with Rolfston in the mating ceremony, but also through turning. Our paranormal family will grow tonight, and I personally think she is going to be a great addition."

"I don't think so, Emmaline," a new voice sneered. Everyone turned around to stare at the man standing at the back of the group.

Rolf moved to stand slightly in front of his mother and Shaye. It gave enough cover that Shaye could get her dagger out and Tess could grab a few of the small potion bottles she had hidden in the pockets of her skirt. He knew Tess was also wearing a conch belt that she had customized to have a small removeable potion bottle hidden in the center of each decorative metal conch. It was a thing of beauty that she and Ian had come up with. You would never know just looking at her that she was armed with so many potions. Her other family members in the crowd were wearing something similar.

"Hello, father. Have you come to wish us a happy mating?" Rolf asked, trying to give everyone time to get ready.

"No," he replied simply.

"You can leave now and just walk away. You can leave us alone and nothing more has to come of this," Rolf tried to reason with his father one more time.

"I don't think so. Your powers are getting to be an annoyance to me. If you won't join with me, then I'll have to remove you. It's a shame I wasted so much time on you. I'll have to start again," Vladimir lamented. His mind was clearly not right. His need for power was too strong.

"I don't want anything to do with your plan. I am quite content here. I don't need to rule over everyone, or to support your need to subjugate people."

"You always were weak, no ambition," his father spat at him as he walked closer. "Surprisingly hard to kill though. I thought that by distracting your human at her work by sending all those people to the clinic at the last full moon, that she would be too drained at the end of the day and wouldn't be able to save you. You also cost me a couple of good people since Dan and Roger are still on the run from the Wardens. It doesn't matter. Once I kill your mate, there will be no one to heal you as I finally kill you. I brought a few friends with me. They're itching for a good fight, but at least they'll have fun killing everyone around you. It's a shame your mating day won't happen. You really should have been better prepared for an attack."

Rolf nodded. He watched as the men who came with

Vlad surrounded his friends. "You're right. It would have been a blood bath if we hadn't anticipated this. However, we did, and we are prepared," Rolf concluded as he drew his blade that had been hidden in a back holster under his cloak.

There was a rush of sound as Rolf's allies all drew their weapons. It was a mix of swords, daggers, and shifted creatures. Vlad's face turned almost purple with rage. He had been so convinced that he would have an easy victory. He rushed forward in anger, his own blades drawn, a sword in one hand and a dagger in the other. Rolf moved to meet him, keeping Vlad farther away from his mother and mate. He could sense that Doc had come out onto the patio and was prepared to help if needed.

Sam's wolf stood nearby, fangs bared, and the ruff of his fur raised. His wolf was large and powerful; his muscles bunching together as he leapt onto an enemy vampire who was trying to circle behind Rolf. The vampire grabbed at him, pushing him away, but Sam's claws dug into the man's stomach, giving him enough of a grip to pull himself forward and tear out his throat.

Ian and Berkley were trying to stay close to Emma and the girls. They were fighting together, working as a well-coordinated pair. Every so often there was a blur of movement, when Ian would use his speed to dart forward to help defend someone else before returning to his mate's side.

'*Concentrate on your father, Mate,*' Shaye scolded as Vlad's sword got a little too close to Rolf. The sounds of metal striking metal and yells, along with grunts of pain, soon filled the clearing. Rolf could scent the blood that was being spilled. He saw a shadow overhead; it was too big to be Gawain. Kicking out with a foot, he pushed his father back allowing Rolf a split second to glance upward. Definitely not Gawain; that was a dragon circling above the clearing. It was too tight of a space to use dragon's fire without hitting both its allies and its foes. Rolf had no idea whose side it was on; he didn't personally know any dragons. He looked back down quickly and saw that his father had dropped his dagger in order to swing his sword with both hands at Rolf's neck. Quickly raising his own sword, Rolf grunted at the impact as the blades met.

"I hope you had a good pre-mating night," Vlad taunted, trying to distract Rolf. "I have someone moving up on your little human right now to finish her off."

"We did have a good night, thanks for asking, father. I believe my mate can defend herself," Rolf added as he ducked and swung his sword at Vlad's middle. His allies had been more than a match for the people Vlad brought and he could see the battle was going to be a quick one. Many of Vlad's followers were ill-prepared for a fair fight. A few had run off as soon as they realized that Rolf's group was armed. His friends were steadily defeating their foes.

Rolf heard Shaye's quick inhale of breath and turned his head to look. A man towered over her with his blade drawn and pointed at her neck. Shaye's dagger wouldn't be long enough to reach him. She quickly leaned to the side and ducked. Lunging forward, she stabbed the guy in the stomach and quickly darted away as Tess threw a potion at him. As the liquid hit him, he screamed and dropped to the ground. Once he was down, the screams stopped and he didn't move again. Rolf saw someone sneaking behind the girls. He started to shout a warning when suddenly a huge tail dropped down from the air and swatted the enemy away.

'Rolf, turn around!' Shaye yelled as she ran toward him. She took her dagger and threw it past his shoulder.

"Stupid bitch," he heard his father grunt in pain.

Turning, he barely ducked in time to miss his father's blade. As he parried and pushed back, he saw Shaye's dagger buried in his father's shoulder. Shaye joined him, grabbing the sword from the fallen Vlad minion on the ground, fighting his father as a team. As his father's arm swung his blade toward them, Shaye buried her sword in his gut while Rolf lunged forward driving his sword into his father's heart. "She's not my *human* anymore. She's turned already. Goodbye, father." Rolf used all his strength to twist the blade, shredding the heart and killing his father.

As the body fell to the ground, Rolf shouted, "Vlad is dead! Leave now or die with him." Most of Vlad's followers fled, but a few were too caught up in their blood lust. They were soon dispatched as well.

His mother came over to him, appearing unharmed. Emma had her own weapons in her hands. "We better make sure the bastard is really dead," she muttered. She stood over his body, using her dagger to cut out the remains of his heart. Dropping it next to his body, she swung her sword as hard as she could, decapitating the head. Her family watched as she proceeded to use her blade to remove each of his limbs. She cursed Vlad as she decimated his body. "Piece of shit, son of a bitch. Taking things from other people that weren't yours. Hurting people just for your own pleasure. Taking my baby from me, trying to turn him to be like you, then trying to kill him when he was a good soul. Never again. We're making sure you can't hurt anyone else. Maybe some fire as well," she muttered, looking around. "Hey, you! Dragon! Can you burn this for me?" Emma asked.

"Mom, are you alright?" Rolf asked, concerned. His mother rarely cursed, and he had never seen her get this violent.

"Yes, just making sure the asshole can't come back," Emma replied calmly, panting a bit from the exertion.

The dragon landed. "If you get all the bodies together, I can burn them all at once."

"Let me check with the Sheriff first. I'm not sure if we're supposed to follow any certain Warden rules for this," Rolf replied. He planned on living in this town for a very long time and would rather not piss off the local Warden. He stepped off to the side to make the phone call.

'Do you think Mom's alright?' Rolf asked Shaye as he dialed.

'Yes, I do. I think she experienced trauma and then years of fear of Vlad. She didn't have the strength to fight him on her own, but she could help today. I think she is getting closure in a very physical way. She needs to know that Vlad can't hurt her or you anymore,' Shaye responded.

"Sheriff is on his way," he said, rejoining the group. "He just wants to document and then said he would be happy for the assistance in the clean up," he told the dragon.

Minutes later, the Sheriff came up the walk. "Well, this is a bit of a mess. I'm glad to see y'all are alright. I just need to make a note of who was here with Vlad."

"There were a few that left, but someone can probably give you some sort of description of them."

"Anyone on your side seriously injured?" he asked.

Rolf took stock of his group. "Nothing life-threatening," he replied. "Doc is treating the injured on the patio."

"Thank you for coming, Sheriff," Shaye added. "I'm going to go help Doc."

"Ma'am." He tipped his hat at her. "Duncan, I hear you're going to help with clean up?" he asked the dragon. "I'm glad you were able to make it."

"I wouldn't have missed it," the dragon replied. "I've been wanting to settle up with Vlad for years after he killed my sister."

Rolf held out his hand. "I'm sorry my father did that to you. Thank you for your help today, especially protecting my mate."

"Vlad was bad news. We all heard about how you were turned and how you turned away from him. What your father did is no reflection on you. I'm glad I could help out some good people."

After the bodies were gathered and the Sheriff had enough information for his file, Duncan let loose a huge flame, cremating the remains. Berkley quickly threw up a small magical dome around the burial pyre to keep the flames and smell contained.

Shaye stood by Doc's side, handing him a prepared suture set. There weren't as many injuries as she feared; some stitches, a few burns, and there was a concussion. Doc stitched them up and she sent a tendril of healing to each patient to speed up their recovery. She healed the concussion right away; Gawain had been hit while he was flying and smacked into a tree.

Emma came over to Doc and let him hold her as she watched the flames. "It's over now," she said in relief. "He can't hurt us anymore." Once everything had burned down to ashes, which only took a few minutes, Emma shook herself off and gave Doc a kiss on the cheek. "I'm going to go bring the food out. Everyone is going to need the energy after fighting."

Shaye watched after her.

"She'll be fine," she heard Doc tell her. "She just needs

time to realize she is free now. No more boogeyman waiting in the shadows."

Shaye nodded. "I'm going to go help her bring stuff out." Walking toward the house, she saw Ian starting a fire in the outdoor fireplace. Berkley spun him around and kissed him as soon as the fire caught. Tess had her legs wrapped around Sam's waist peppering his face with kisses.

They had placed a few large folding tables around the patio to act as triage tables if needed and dinner tables once everyone was patched up. It was going to be a casual dinner, but they wanted to feed their friends. Between Emma and Shaye, it only took a few trips to bring out the slow cookers. They placed them on a table by the house with bowls and spoons. Shaye brought out baskets filled with breads and butter. There were a few coolers around the patio containing drinks. Once everyone had eaten, they could find places for people to sleep if they wanted to stay. They had some room in the house, some at the hotel in town, and they had some tents and air mattresses as well. She had already placed an order with the town's bakery for a large donut and danish order that she could pick up in the morning.

Rolf was exhausted. He was relieved his father was dead. He had watched to make sure the body was completely destroyed, no chance of him recovering. The Sheriff stayed for some dinner and said he would submit the final report, but that there wouldn't be any issues. They had had a few minor injuries, but nothing severe, which he was incredibly grateful for. His mother seemed to have had a weight taken off her. She still wasn't ready for mating yet, but he did notice that she would pat Doc's arm as she went by or would hold his hand for short periods of time. He knew Doc would let her heal and would not rush her into a mating. He would be a great stepfather, he thought and then snorted. Who would have thought he would get a new father figure at two hundred and four years old?

Most of the friends who had come today had stayed for dinner and conversation after the fight. Some had wandered back into town to get a hotel room, and some had already moved on. They did have a few staying in the backyard, including Duncan the Dragon. He found the alliteration much funnier than he should, Rolf told himself. Everyone was already in their beds, and he obviously needed sleep. He was too wound up to sleep yet and was sitting in the library just staring at the shelves.

'*Mate, come to bed,*' Shaye told him as she walked into the room. '*It's late and you need to sleep.*'

'*I can't turn my mind off,*' he admitted. '*My brain will eventually calm down and I'll come up. You go ahead to bed. I don't want to keep you up.*'

'*I have a better idea,*' Shaye told him as she pulled him out of the chair and led him up the stairs.

EPILOGUE

"Love, what do you think of keeping everyone?" Rolf asked Shaye as they sat reading. It had been about a week since the fight with his father and things had calmed down. They were getting into a new routine with Ian and Emma joining their household. Thanksgiving was soon and Shaye, Tess, and Emma had all sat down to plan the huge feast. They had sent an open invitation to friends to stop in. He didn't want anyone to be alone on the holiday, especially those who had risked their lives to help them when they needed it.

"Keep everyone? What do you mean?" Shaye asked with a grin. She had an inkling, thanks to Tess's dreams. She had just been waiting for him to play catch-up.

"I want to formalize our Clan. Everyone we love is here. I know we have a few that travel a lot for work like Gawain and possibly Ian, but this could be their home base. If they all start having families, we can build on the property and still be able to keep everyone under the protection of the ward. The town seems to enjoy having new residents, plus they bring in more income for the locals by shopping in town and if they would want to open their own stores, more tourists might visit. Ian can open a blacksmith and/or leather store. Gawain could always open a history museum or something if he wanted. The humans would probably think it was a curiosity museum, but the paranormals would know it's real. I would have loved to have been able to go learn about the vampire beginnings and what was the truth versus what my father told me to keep me in line. I don't want to take over the town, but I think we can beneficially co-exist with it."

"What goes into making a Clan?" she asked.

"There's some paperwork to fill out. Mostly so that if the Wardens come across a troublemaker, they know who he or she belongs to. Some punishments are handled by the Clans, Packs, or family groups. Some are only handled by the Wardens. I can get it started today if everyone agrees," he said eagerly.

"Well, I love the idea. Let's go talk to our family then, hmm?" Shaye pulled him out of the chair. Leaving the library, they headed to where they heard voices. Tess and Emma were in the kitchen, while Sam was trying to sneak pieces of whatever they were making. Doc was reading a medical journal on the couch. Ian and Berkley were sketching out some kind of design.

Rolf cleared his throat. "What does everyone think about me declaring us officially a Clan? We'd keep it here on the house and grounds. It would be inclusive, since we are all different species. If someone new wanted to join, the eight of us would all have input on if they were accepted. You guys would be the Clan Council. If you want to live outside of this house, we can build on the property for whatever you want. We're already looking at building a forge and kiln area for Ian and Berkley, if they can decide on a design."

Berkley spoke up. "We're all in. We talked about it,

and we would love to officially be a family, a Clan." Everyone nodded their agreement.

Rolf sighed in relief. "Great, I'll get the paperwork started today."

"What is the name of the Clan?" his mother asked.

"Welcome, everyone, to the Nightwood Clan," Rolf announced.

NOTE FROM THE AUTHOR

Thank you for reading my book! If you enjoyed the story, please leave a review. Reviews are invaluable to independent authors.

PROLOGUE

Tess was chomping at the bit, as it were. She had her most important belongings packed into the back of her car and could not wait until it was time to leave. Although she was leaving her mom's house, this was not the first time she had moved away from her family. At seventy-five years old, she was an adult in both the human and paranormal world. She had grown up in a small tight-knit community of witches, all of which she was related to in some way or another. It was common for witches to live in huge family groups, but Tess had always wanted to explore the world, meet other paranormals. Being the youngest, with a bit of an age gap between her and her siblings, she never felt the need to stay close to home. Something kept drawing her away. Her mother especially did not understand it but had reluctantly accepted Tess's traveling when it was around the New Orleans and Texas areas, where there were groups of her father's family.

When Tess reached New Orleans about twelve years

ago, she had only been planning on a short visit. The short visit had turned into a seven-year stay. During her first couple of days in the city, she had met Shaye, a young human starting at the college. After Tess's magic had literally pushed her toward Shaye, causing Tess to trip in front of her at a coffee shop, Shaye had held out a hand to help steady her. As their hands touched, Tess's magic had lit up. The quick premonition showed their friendship intertwined for the rest of their lives, a friendship that was more like being part of a family. A quick glance at Shaye's aura showed that while she had an enormous natural gift for healing, it unfortunately came with an empathetic side that she could not shield herself from very well. Over the years, Tess had helped teach her a few basics on shielding and coping with her gifts.

Unfortunately, while Shaye had a strong healing gift, she had no other knowledge of the magical or paranormal world. Tess's family rules forbade her from telling outsiders about her heritage. There was a reason of course; throughout the centuries, there had been several good witches who had been killed due to fear and misunderstanding, including her own ancestors. Even their friend Ian, who was a vampire, had not told Shaye the truth yet. Although she was not sure why he was keeping his paranormal status a secret.

Her magic often gave her pushes or premonitions, usually in dream form. While they helped show her snippets of the future, they rarely showed all of the situation. Her latest dream showed Shaye moving in with a vampire boyfriend. On the plus side, Shaye was now exposed to the paranormal world, so Tess could finally confess the only secret she had kept from Shaye. From a more questionable angle, Tess wasn't sure what had made Shaye move in with a boyfriend so quickly. Shaye's dating experience wasn't extensive, but each one had ended poorly. There had been one or two that had stopped after date one. Shaye wasn't one to jump into bed with someone right away when dating due to her gifts, so when she wouldn't go home with them after the first date, they often didn't call back. There were a couple who lasted a few months, but those ended when they found out she had a bit of a gift. One guy had called her a freak, the other had tried to exploit her gift for his own monetary gain. That guy had been extremely persistent even after their breakup, but after a secret visit from Ian he finally left Shaye alone. Tess may have also created a spell to make sure he couldn't get within touching distance of Shaye again, her own version of a restraining order.

Shaye's family was nonexistent, so Tess and Ian made sure to always remember her birthday and Christmas, even if they wouldn't be together. She had invited Shaye home for a few holidays over the years and she knew Ian had done the same. Tess suspected that Ian had started to draw back a little bit because he wasn't aging and did not want to cause suspicion. Tess had also dreaded the day that she would have to distance herself from her friend. Without the two of them, Shaye's support network would become extremely small, and it would have broken something inside Tess to hurt her friend that way. When she had the dream showing Shaye with a paranormal boyfriend, Tess knew the moment had come to reunite with her friend and to confess her secret. Even if Shaye stayed human, once Tess was able to tell her she was a witch, they could be friends for the rest of her life. Tess had always hoped that Shaye would find a paranormal mate so that she wouldn't have to watch her friend age and die so soon. With the danger lurking in the back- ground of the dream, Tess had started making plans to move. The dreams didn't show a definite time, so she would feel better once she was within touching distance of Shaye and could help protect her.

While Tess was extremely excited for this new journey, her family was not as eager. Most of her mom's family all lived in the witch-only neighborhood, including all her siblings. They kept trying to tell Tess that moving to a smaller community, one with limited access to other witches, was a bad idea. Of course, they forgot that she had lived on her own for quite a few years already. Tess chose to believe in her dreams. She knew that the town Shaye's boyfriend Rolf called home would soon be hers as well. It called to her.

"Do you have everything?" her mom asked for the fourth time.

"Yes, Mom. I have my spells, all the supplies I might need, some potion bottles, and two weeks' worth of clothes, plus my winter gear. I am seventy-five, I know how to pack," Tess assured her, and laughed.

"I know," her mom admitted. "I just do not like you being so far away. You are the baby of the family. I am going to miss you."

Tess rolled her eyes. "I have lived apart from you before. Besides, it's only a couple of hours away." She gave her mom a hug. "Shaye is like a sister to me—"

"Thanks a lot," one of her older sisters yelled from somewhere in the house. She thought it was Theresa. "If only you had more of those."

Tess rolled her eyes. With seven older siblings, Tess had been a late-in-life surprise. Her mom was one hundred and sixty years old and had most of her kids quickly. First it was triplet boys, then a boy and girl set of twins, then another boy/girl set of twins, and finally a few (more like twenty-five) years later came Tess. Her mom had thought she was done having kids at the age of eighty-five before Tess came around. The large age gap between siblings meant that while Tess was part of her large family, she often felt separated from her brothers and sisters. Out of all her biological siblings, she was probably closest with Merri. The youngest set of twins had not mated yet and still lived at home, so Tess had interacted more with Stefan and Merri than the rest of her siblings. Heck, her oldest brother Tim had his first child when Tess was only a year old.

However, even though she had been much older than Shaye when they had met, Tess had felt instantly connected and closer to her than to most of her siblings. Tess was really looking forward to this move; friends, new family, and lots of different types of paranormals to interact with. She currently worked in medical coding, since it allowed her to work from home and had some flexibility to the workday. She had maintained her North Carolina and Tennessee nursing licenses as well, so she should be able to make a life in the town quite easily.

"Alright, Mom. It is time for me to go. I will text you when I get there." She gave her mom another hug before heading out the front door. Honestly, her mom made a big deal now, but ten minutes after Tess was gone, she would be fine. Having all your kids, grandkids, and any other relative living within walking distance meant that her mom always had someone stopping over.

"Tess," she heard Merri call out from the doorway. "I made this for you, for safe travels and no car problems," she said, handing her a keychain. It had some protective crystals and a spell woven into it.

"Thank you, Merri." Tess hugged her sister. "You will have to come visit. I know it is going to be amazing, and I think you will like it. I see a huge library somewhere in town and a cute bookstore we could explore." Tess would have to make more of an effort to keep in contact with her sister. Merri was quiet and liked to stay home, whereas

Tess liked exploring and socializing with all different kinds of people. While they did not hang out a lot, Merri was still the closest sibling relationship she had. They did share a love of books though and word games on their phones.

"That does sound fun," Merri agreed and smiled.

Tess climbed into her car, programmed the GPS, and left into the sunrise. She couldn't wait.

ABOUT THE AUTHOR

I have loved reading since I was a child. I also enjoy baking, photography, and seeing new things. My favorite books are romances with a happily ever-after. The world is a crazy place. Sometimes escaping into a great book is the only way I can truly relax. Happily-ever-after is my favorite type of book, so my stories will end with a HEA, even if the road is a little bumpy getting there. I travel a lot, but currently reside in the Midwest with my family.

Stay up to date with news, book release dates, special promotions and adventures, by visiting my website and social media pages.

www.HarperDakota.com
Harper's Readers Group

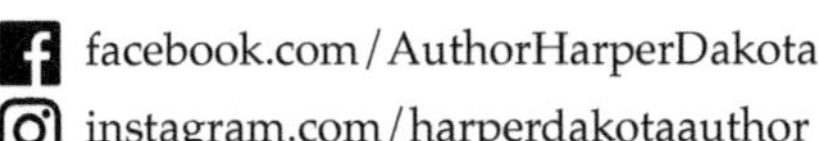

facebook.com/AuthorHarperDakota
instagram.com/harperdakotaauthor

ALSO BY HARPER DAKOTA

Nightwood Clan Series

Bite Me Again

A Hairy Situation

Pointed Love

www.ingramcontent.com/pod-product-compliance
Lightning Source LLC
Chambersburg PA
CBHW070653010826
48975CB00013B/1087